*Runagates in Scarceness*

# Runagates in Scarceness

## A Holy Mystery

O. C. EDWARDS JR.

RESOURCE *Publications* • Eugene, Oregon

RUNAGATES IN SCARCENESS
A Holy Mystery

Resource Publications
An Imprint of Wipf and Stock Publishers
199 W. 8th Ave., Suite 3
Eugene, OR 97401

www.wipfandstock.com

ISBN 13: 978-1-62564-359-9

Manufactured in the USA

Dedicated to
My Former Students
Who Have Taught Me
So Much

# Preface

This novel was written in 1980 and revised slightly for this edition. Thus it displays attitudes common for its time and for the period in which the story is set, some of which have changed markedly in the years since, e.g., those toward homosexuality. To alter these would make them anachronistic so they have been left intact, but they should not be taken as indicative of my stance today.

The resuscitation of the manuscript owes a great deal to a number of persons whose names will not be given for fear of omitting some and slighting persons to whom I am deeply grateful. It is hoped that they all know who they are and will feel acknowledged by this statement. The two exceptions I will make to this anonymity are my copyeditor Lorrie Cooper and my wife Jane, who has put up with me for fifty-six years and supported me in all my endeavors. I am afraid she is guilty of enabling.

# 1

While the bell was calling the community to prayer, Canon Bothwell vested to officiate at Evensong. Over his cassock and surplice he adjusted his academic hood and pulled his black scarf over his head, checking the mirror to make sure its ends hung down evenly in front. Though the full-length mirror in the vesting room had been losing mercury off its back for most of the hundred thirty years since the seminary was founded, and its reflective surface was, as usual, further diminished by a layer of dust on its surface, it nevertheless returned enough of an image for Bothwell to be amused by the memory of overhearing a student describe his appearance as that of a plump icon. His hair did indeed recede over a forehead that bulged as though (they had said) his skull had difficulty in containing his brain. Even the un-Byzantine tortoiseshell of his owlish glasses contributed to the overall numinous effect, and his goatee and moustache could have been modeled on those of St. John Chrysostom. Only the protuberance of the well-bred paunch billowing his surplice conflicted with the gaunt image of Eastern asceticism. A mere flick of his preaching tabs was all that remained to render him decently habited to officiate at the evening service.

Leaving the oily smell of the dark oak vestment cases and making his way across floors worn uneven by generations of student feet, he left the sacristy and entered the place of worship. Passing alongside the altar area, he went behind the long choir where the student body members faced each another across the central aisle and then turned to walk between the shallow nave where visitors sat (called "the court of the gentiles") and the back of the stalls facing the altar. That row of stalls seated the faculty, who maintained their surveillance to ensure that all was done "decently and in order."

Reverencing the altar, he settled on his knees in the Sub-dean's stall, assuring himself by a quick check that his Prayer Book, hymnal, and psalter were marked at the proper places. Then he buried his head in his hands, using the "shampoo position" favored by many Anglicans as the appropriate posture for addressing their God. The act of vesting had helped release him from the wandering and repetitious discussions of the afternoon's faculty meeting, so his devotions now were not so much explicit instructions to the Deity as returning awareness of the Presence in which he and all creatures always dwell.

The student organist in the loft finally completed the prelude, a showy piece chiefly notable for its variations in volume and tempo. Bothwell's recitation of the opening words of the evening office managed to restore the mood of recollection that had been blasted by the organ's blare. After twenty-two years at Chase Clergy Training College (this archaic British designation being one of a number of his affectations that the founder had imposed on the institution), the Canon knew all the words of the Prayer Book's sixteenth-century translation of the Psalms and the tones to which they were set. This knowledge freed him to relax in his seat while chanting with the community and at the same time safely glance around the chapel without endangering the flow of plainsong from his lips.

When in the 1830s Bishop Philander Chase became disgruntled with Kenyon and Bexley Hall, the college and seminary he had founded in Ohio, he had returned to his English friends to seek funds for erecting in the wilderness of Indiana yet another school for the prophets. This chapel was the first fruits of those efforts. In accord with the tastes of its ducal donor, the building was chaste Georgian. Large windows with rounded tops and clear glass panes let in what remained of the winter evening light, fading light that had its life prolonged and sustained for a moment longer by the white paint covering the wainscoting and the gated period pews that boxed in their inhabitants. Even the triple-decker pulpit of the period had been retained, as had also the tablets above the holy table setting forth the Ten Commandments, the Creed, and the Lord's Prayer.

Large brass chandeliers with more arms than octopi held aloft candles, although they were now fake and wired. The only ripple in this serene pond of Georgian order was an immense brass sanctuary lamp that hung from the ceiling on a long chain, the gift of a turn-of-the-century patron who often raided Europe for pious objects with which to ornament and edify the seminary. The Gothic exuberance of both its design and devotional style was foreign in this locale of good taste and restraint, and the rest of the building seemed to hold aloof from it in a typically British response to a foreigner. Since the sacrament was not reserved at Chase anyway, the flickering light was frustrated in its efforts to pay tribute to the Eucharistic presence of Christ.

The chanting community had already expressed in the words of the sixty-eighth Psalm its willingness to let God arise and his enemies be scattered, when Canon Bothwell had his attention distracted from an inspection of the student body by a phrase from the sixth verse, glorious in its archaic verbiage: "letteth the runagates continue in scarceness." Would those who were busy revising the Book of Common Prayer merely update *runagates* into *renegades,* or did the Hebrew mean something else? At any rate, renegades were pretty scarce around there, although Bothwell thought he had heard once that Chase's Wisconsin rival, Nashotah House, had been used as a hideout by a Chicago gangster during Prohibition. Nothing so exotic had ever happened at Chase. He had long since lost his naiveté about seminarians and knew they had most of the weaknesses of non-seminarians, but usually these foibles did not manifest themselves so dramatically and publicly. Runagates were scarce at the Clergy Training College.

Later, after he had unvested, Bothwell walked down the sidewalk connecting the sacristy with the arched walkway between the chapel and the Green Building. The chapel windows were dark now, except for the small round one looking out from the loft where the organist was plotting his next assault on the ears of the faithful. Standing under the arch, Bothwell waited for Tom Wright, the professor of pastoral theology, with whom he always had a glass of sherry after Evensong on days the faculty met. Their merger of clinical views with historical interpretation was usually livelier and probably more productive than the session inspiring it. While he waited for Tom, who was either picking up a book from the library, meeting the need of a student who had waylaid him, or doing whatever else was keeping him, the Canon looked out over the campus. Night had fallen now, and the campus was illuminated by lamps hung over doorways and set on posts along the walks.

The chapel had been the first of the seminary buildings, and no other permanent ones were erected until the Dean in the 1890s had convinced some industrialist Episcopalians in Indianapolis that their own *amour propre* required that their clergy be trained in a setting of dignity. One of them knew that the architect to commission was H.H. Richardson, who had recently given ponderous nobility to houses and depots, churches and banks. Since the chapel had been erected at the back of the block, Richardson created a layout similar to the shape of a tuning fork, with the chapel serving as the handle. The Dean had two buildings put down on what remained of the block, each on a prong of the fork, and connected by arcades at their north ends with the front of the chapel. The two buildings, which faced each other over a wide quadrangle, were constructed of different materials. The building to the east of the chapel, housing administrative offices, class rooms, and library, was made of Indiana limestone embellished with marble, granite, and a little brick; and it was always referred to as "The School." Its opposite number, the Green Building, owed its inspiration to the muse responsible for lodges being erected at that time in national parks; its materials were shingles, logs, and rough lumber, all of which were stained to the color giving the building its name. Here the single students lived, ate, and had such facilities as they enjoyed for entertainment, exercise, and the household chores of bachelors.

Obscured by the arcade and wrapped in his black cloak, Bothwell watched his breath turn to fog in the cool night air. His attention was arrested from this inspection by the sound of footsteps from the direction of the chapel. Turning, he saw the back of a tall young man whose legs were khaki stovepipes emerging beneath a B-24 flight jacket. The lamp over the door highlighted a blond crew cut, and Bothwell knew from that and from the figure's athletic grace that the celebrity of the Junior class (as first-year students were called) was exiting the building: Seth Clarke, late first lieutenant in the Army's Special Forces and Medal of Honor winner in a war in which there appeared little honor to be gained.

Clarke turned neither to the right nor to the left but instead walked toward the dark, unpaved middle section of the quad. Bothwell looked in the direction the young man was headed and saw the person Clarke was moving to intercept. Even in the reduced light Bothwell could see that she was dressed with chic that seldom graced the campus of CCTC. While most of the student wives still wore miniskirts, this young woman was clad in a tweed jacket and flannel trousers. Something about the way the bottom of the jacket swirled reminded Bothwell of the fox-hunting crowd when he was at Cambridge, but a style utterly masculine on them acquired an exquisitely feminine aspect on her. When she emerged into light, Bothwell recognized her as Clarke's wife, Sheila, who was no less a celebrity, having been Miss Illinois. At Atlantic City she had won the swimsuit competition and was generally admitted to have been the nearest thing to a real beauty there, but rumors leaked that she had not been in the running for the friendship award. Her talent had been dramatic reading, which is to say she had no talent. In reality, it was as a couple that Sheila and Seth were best known. Their meeting at a bond rally when Clarke was back in the States to be decorated by the President, their whirlwind courtship, and their honeymoon cut short by emergency orders had been one of the few romantic things to fill space in newspapers otherwise devoted to accounts of unavailing warfare abroad, riots at home, and gloom and violence everywhere.

"Did you come to meet me?" Clarke called to his wife as they neared each another. Bothwell thought his voice sounded both a little surprised and a little hopeful.

"No, I didn't really expect to see you. I left a note explaining." Sheila changed course enough that she could walk past without stopping.

"But what about supper?"

"It's on the stove. All you have to do is heat it twenty minutes at 350 degrees and peel the foil off."

"Not another of those damn TV dinners!"

Sheila had already reached the bottom steps of the chapel. She stopped, turned toward him, and said, "I'm sorry, I can't be the breadwinner and the maid and the cook and everything else. Besides, I have to make my meditation. Don't think that because you are the seminarian, you are the only one in the family who can have a spiritual life." With that she ran up the steps and entered the chapel. Seth walked off into the dark, hands in his pockets, his shoulders rounded, his athlete's stride reduced to a shuffle.

Later, seated in the Wright's living room, Bothwell was warmed not only by the roaring fire, but also by the room's comfort and the welcome of Tom and his wife Mary, an artist. Less formal than his own parlor and less orderly as well, the room nevertheless made him feel very much at home. The Wrights' concern for the comfort of their guests was summed up for Bothwell in the way every place to sit was within easy reaching distance of a surface on which to rest a glass or an ashtray. The room's furnishings were eclectic, chosen for comfort rather than period, and carrying associations with the places the Wrights had lived. The pictures on the walls were divided between Mary Wright's work and that of friends with whom she had exchanged pieces. Her own represented an earlier period when she had done landscapes in an impressionistic style. Nowhere to be seen was her current work, canvases on which were juxtaposed bands of color only slightly modeled or shaded with the economy, order, and aesthetic satisfaction of a Japanese garden. "It's not relaxing," she explained to Bothwell, "to sit surrounded by my current explorations in style."

This evening it did not take long to dispose of the faculty meeting. The Dean had acted very much in character. For The Very Reverend J. Stanley

Huston, programs or projects were to be evaluated not so much for their improvement of students' preparation for ministry as for their effectiveness in giving the world the impression that the Clergy Training College was in the vanguard of the seminary world. This preference for appearance over substance had once been labeled by Bothwell as the window dressing approach to theological education. "To be rather than to seem" was not a motto that Huston was ever likely to adopt.

Bothwell was still disturbed by the scene that he had witnessed while waiting for Tom, disturbed and a little embarrassed at having been an eavesdropper on a conversation that should have been private, although it was conducted in a tone of voice easily audible from fifteen yards away. As a bachelor he had an idealized view of what marital relations should be, and he knew that parishioners expected, however unfairly, that the marriage in the rectory would be better than that in their own houses. It was natural for him to share what he had heard with his friends, not in any spirit of gossip that delights in the discovery of feet of clay, but in a pastoral concern for the development of a student who would someday bear the responsibility of ministering to others. And Tom had come to the seminary from parish ministry rather than academia.

"You know, Rod," he said, "I haven't really gotten to know the Clarkes since I don't teach Juniors. But let me suggest what might be going on with this couple. When my mind is unhampered by facts, I am free to perform great feats of interpretation. There is a guy at Harvard named Harvey Cox who wrote a fascinating book a couple of years ago called *The Secular City*. I make all of my parish administration students read it. In it Cox discusses beauty pageants, especially Miss America. He proposes that Miss America and Hugh Heffner's Playboy function in our society like goddesses and gods did in primitive societies, providing models for the members of the society and personifying and authenticating its value structure. The Playboy and 'the Girl,' as he calls her, epitomize our society's devotion to leisure and consumerism. Here, let me read you a bit," Tom said as he unfolded his lank limbs and moved to one of the bulging bookcases.

Watching his friend as he stretched his long, big-boned fingers to select a volume, pull it down, and flip quickly through to find a place, Bothwell thought that there was something Lincolnesque about Tom, although it was a resemblance in type rather that in detail, since his features had a different sort of homely beauty. His mouth was as mobile as Honest Abe's, his nose as hooked, and he had as many moles; but his head was rounder, his brow slanted, and while it was not weak, his chin did recede.

"Here it is," he said. "Listen to this. 'In Miss America's glowingly healthy smile, her openly sexual but officially virgin figure, and in the brand-name gadgets around her, she personifies the stunted aspirations and ambivalent fears of her culture. There she goes, she is your ideal.' How's that? Maybe Sheila's life of glamorous consumerism didn't prepare her for being the wife of a seminarian."

"I've read that, too, Tom," Bothwell replied. "I found Cox's analysis very interesting, but not convincing. I was at the Brady's for dinner one night several years ago when the Miss America pageant was held, and we watched it on TV. While anyone with a brain in his head can figure out that the main activity of the reigning Miss America will be to advertise consumer products, few people ever attend the events at which she does that advertising. Far more watch the pageant on TV, and it is in the context of the pageant that they understand her. For all of the promotion of products done by former Misses America during the commercial breaks, the contestants seem removed from it all.

"The social value that she embodies is our 'look but don't touch' approach to sex, in which we say that all of our post-pubescent children should be hyper-developed in their secondary sexual characteristics, but not do anything with them. I've heard that the Bunnies in Playboy clubs are not even allowed to date the customers. We live in an atmosphere of great erotic stimulation for the young and yet permit them no outlets except fantasy and autoeroticism, practices that are hidden in the dark. Cox should have developed his point about the virgin goddess instead. And I would not be surprised if our Miss Sheila has not grown up with the idea that the rules call for everyone to admire her looks, but no one to make demands on her. That's at least the way that it looks to me at six p.m. on Monday, this fifth day of January, in 1970."

Mary had sat quietly listening to this conversation with a bemused expression and finally spoke up.

"Oh, you men! Long academic speeches that have nothing to do with the way people actually live. Don't you know what it's like for those girls living over at the Hutches? Most of them drive miles to work after they've prepared breakfast for the family and gotten the kids on the school bus. Then they drive back at the end of a long day to cook supper and spend their evenings with housecleaning, laundry, and mothering while their husbands are off with their noses in books and their heads in a theological air that is not sullied by the sordid realities of daily life. I don't blame Sheila. I would rebel too."

"Except that you haven't," Tom said. "It has amazed me that for thirty years you have made a wonderful home for the kids and me and seldom complained that my long hours kept me from bearing my load at home."

"But you've never acted as though it was only what was expected of me, and that it was beneath you. And you have always recognized that painting is as much of a vocation for me as the priesthood is for you, even if we couldn't arrange for me to spend as much time at it. I still think you had better have those boys read Betty Friedan, because there is a new day coming. Yes, and the two of you need to prepare your colleagues for the day when they will have women students."

Like many artists, Mary showed great interest in the design and fabric texture of her clothes, but she never let concern for the well-cut lines of a garment override considerations of comfort and practicality. She had too strong of a sense of her own identity and worth to squeeze her ample torso into girdles. Her hair dressers had tried to persuade her to do something with her nicely textured hair other than the pageboy cut she had worn for years, but she told them she did not want to waste time fooling with it. "What a truly good person she is," Bothwell thought as she brought over the decanter to offer another drink. Although tempted, he remembered his housekeeper's dinner orders.

"No, thank you," he said, "while my bond to Katrina is commercial rather than sacramental, I have learned not to abuse her patience. She told me not later than six-thirty, and it's almost that now. Besides, I've got to introduce the meaning of history to the Juniors tomorrow, so I must be fortified by preparation and sleep."

Rising from his chair, he added, "I'm glad that there is one place on this campus where I can be confident that something offered as sherry will be from Spain. There are many excellent American wines, but the most expensive domestic sherry does not taste like the same beverage as the cheapest import from Jerez." He wrapped his cloak around him, pecked Mary on the cheek, and left.

# 2

Roderick Bothwell removed his handkerchief to wipe chalk dust from his hands, hating not only the gritty feel of it on his fingers but also the awareness that he dare not touch anything for fear of leaving a white smudge. Turning to the lectern at his desk, he grasped the lapels of his gown. New students at Chase had to learn from oral tradition that his was not the robe of someone holding an American Master's degree, but instead what Cambridge doctors wore for occasions not considered ceremonial. Faculty at the seminary still wore gowns for class and chapel from their Anglophile inheritance as Episcopalians, even though the students wore them only in chapel, one of the fruits so far of the student protest movement at the Clergy Training College.

He was nearing the end of his lecture, sketching in the various contemporary schools of historiography. Some still practiced "the great man" interpretation while others went in for social history. Some historians understood everything in terms of the categories of Freud, while others used those of Marx. Collingwood had said that events must be credible as the acts of human agents. Now there were many who called themselves "revisionists" who satirized the work of those they called "Whig" historians, scholars who viewed evolution in society from authoritarian monarchies to the rise of the modern democratic state as progress. The revisionists called attention to the dark side of American history, arguing that its past was devoted unrelentingly to the exploitation of blacks, Indians, native peoples in its colonial empire, the poor, and women.

"There have been contributions of undoubted worth from all of these schools," the Canon concluded, "but I must confess that I have serious questions about any method that tries to impose a pattern on the shape of history. This seems to me like knowing what your research will prove before you begin your investigation. Or, to change the metaphor, it seems like a detective's understanding his task to be proving the guilt of a certain suspect rather than finding out who committed the crime. Why bother to go to all the trouble if you know in advance where you are going to end up?

"While we have lost much of our naive confidence in the objectivity of facts, I am nevertheless convinced that there is such a thing as historical evidence, and that if we make our facts fit our theories rather than let our interpretation emerge from our data, we are doomed to willful self-delusion. Collingwood may be right in saying that we have to understand events as the acts of human agents, but often the only access we have to the motives of people is through their external behavior. To return to the analogy of criminal investigation—an analogy that many historians have used to explain their work—no amount of guesswork about motive can ever make up for a lack of material evidence that links the suspect to the crime.

"We ignore physical evidence to our peril. In my courses, therefore, you may expect more respect to be paid to the careful gathering of data than to fashionable theories about what history ought to prove. I hope that this word to the wise will be sufficient for all of you. Now, are there any questions?"

After he clarified the points students knew they had misunderstood, Bothwell retrieved his watch from the lectern and restored it to the lower right pocket of his gray flannel vest, draping the narrow gold watch chain across his dignified midsection and sticking the penknife and Phi Beta Kappa key on its end into the left pocket. Clasping his lecture notes and tucking reference books under his arm, he turned to leave, but a voice from behind stopped him.

"Canon Bothwell, I need to talk to you about that term paper. I've never written one before." It was Seth Clarke.

Bothwell paused, put notes and books back on the lectern, and consulted his datebook. "Are you free this afternoon at three, Mr. Clarke? I could see you then."

"I'll be there. Thank you, sir."

Bothwell headed out the door and toward the stairs at the end of the hall. Students released from class clogged the stairwell. Immediately in front of him was a student draped in a white Mexican poncho with black stripes. The garment had a ceremonial appearance between that of a vestment and a monastic habit. From this costume and his long, wavy, golden hair, Bothwell recognized Sebastian Seymour, the incoming class's self-appointed candidate for guru status. Seymour was saying to a nearby classmate who did not appear particularly interested, "I should have known that simply because it was a class in church history, I could not expect to hear anything spiritual. No one around here seems to recognize that Christianity is a religion, and its history therefore might include something about human efforts to experience the divine."

Bothwell saw the elbow aimed at Seymour's ribs and heard the hiss: "Shut up, you fool! Don't you know he's right behind us?" There was the sound of a sharp intake of breath, and the Canon was gratified to see on the face that jerked around to stare at him an expression other than its customary saccharine simper. The day Seymour had arrived at the school, Bothwell had decided he looked like the pictures of the Sacred Heart seen on pine slabs in dime stores. Saying nothing, Bothwell moved on past him.

When Katrina ushered Seth into his study that afternoon, Bothwell seated him in a leather wingchair facing his own. A cheery fireplace was on one side of them and a leather sofa on the other. These seating accommodations were disposed around a low, square table displaying magazines. The room stretched behind Bothwell to a bay window twelve feet away into which was fitted an enormous roll-top desk of walnut that incorporated a veritable columbarium of pigeonholes. All the wall space not occupied with windows was given over to bookcases, except above the mantle where a colored steel engraving showed The General Theological Seminary as it must have looked when its Hebrew professor, Clement Clarke Moore, was writing *A Visit From St. Nicholas* as a Christmas present for his children. Shields hung on either side of the mantle, one from the University of the South and the other from Jesus College, Cambridge. The only object on the mantle itself was a seventeenth-century Spanish crucifix, an ivory corpus suspended from an ebony cross.

"Sit down, Mr. Clarke, sit down. May I offer you some refreshment? My housekeeper can give you coffee or a soft drink."

"Thank you, sir, but I won't take anything. That sort of thing cuts down on my wind."

Passing over to him a large flint glass compote on which were stacked apples, oranges, bananas, and grapes, Bothwell said, "Then have some fruit. That should be healthful enough for you." After Seth had selected a banana, Bothwell returned the compote to the table and took an orange for himself. Then he removed the penknife from his vest pocket and pulled the longer of the two blades from the thin gold handle. With precision he incised the orange top and bottom, the incisions of the top half offsetting the bottom half incisions. Then with the tip of the blade he began to loosen the skin from the fruit, the skin coming away in one piece in a zig-zag pattern.

Fascinated, Seth said that he had never seen anyone peel an orange that way. Bothwell replied that he had peeled all of his oranges that way since his fifth-grade teacher had described Mercator projection maps as misleading since the earth's surface is spherical. To represent it on a flat page, some maps in their geography book laid it out like an orange peel. He could hardly wait to get home and try it.

"But," he continued, "You did not come to learn about my peculiar orange-peeling habits. You want to discuss term papers."

"Yes, sir. You see, I graduated from Purdue with a major in forestry, and the only history course I had was on the history of forestry. And we did not have to write term papers."

Bothwell thought for a moment. "Was that course only about the attitudes toward the forests and the methods of conservation in the various societies, or did you deal with the economic impact of the kinds of lumber available in various periods? I had a student once who had studied engineering, and the only history course he had taken was the history of science, and the only thing he remembered from it was the name of the inventor of the flush toilet, Sir John Harrington, one of the brightest lights at the court of Queen Elizabeth I."

Seth smiled. "Oh, we dealt with the economic implications, all right. It gave me a new way of looking at trees. I went into forestry because I like the woods. I knew that most of my fellow students were going into one end of the lumber business or another, but I wanted to go into conservation. I spent my summers at Turkey Run State Park as a Junior Ranger, and I hoped to go back permanently after graduation."

"Then you had not yet decided to study for the ministry?"

"No, sir. I received my call when I was in 'Nam. But being a forestry major was not the best seminary preparation imaginable. The guys who majored in liberal arts have a much easier time of it here."

"Well, that may be, but don't despair. You bring to your work a background they lack. Would you like to work on a term paper in which you use what you know about the impact of forestry on an economy to explore how the church in that society was influenced by that economic situation?"

"That sounds like something maybe I could do, and that I would find very interesting."

"Good. You don't happen to read French, do you?"

Seth looked surprised. "I do. My mother believed that knowing French was one of the accomplishments of a gentleman, and she made me start as soon as possible in junior high school. I thought it was sissy stuff and drug my heels on it until three-quarters of the way through the first year, when I discovered that it came easy to me, and I actually liked it. It was one of the things that got me into the Special Forces."

"Wonderful, because there is a school of French historians called the *Annalistes* who believe that history grows out of geography, demography, and economics. One of them, Fernand Braudel, has written a two-volume study on the Mediterranean area in the sixteenth century. We won't be dealing with that period until next year, but his geography holds true for earlier periods. Perhaps you can take his work along with that of Rostovsteff on the social and economic history of the Roman Empire and write about how some economic condition connected with forestry affected the early history of the church. How does that sound?"

"That sounds great, sir. You really have taken a load off my mind. Thanks a lot."

"Oh, you're most welcome. It's what I'm here for. But, if you don't mind, perhaps you can help me."

"I'd be glad to do anything I can."

"I would appreciate your reaction to the discussion in class this morning. It helps me to know what questions are of concern to a number of students, and which are merely the private interests of the individuals asking."

"Well, from various bull sessions and from what I've heard said in courses in the fall semester, I'd say those responses were typical. What really got me angry was Sebastian's remark after class. I was coming along behind you on the way down the stairs, and I heard him. That creep! I would love to take him out and give him a little judo instruction."

"Perhaps he was a little injudicious in his expression or at least in the occasion of it, but you seem to feel strongly about my honor. Is there perhaps some personal animus involved that contributes to the intensity of your response?"

"Yes, sir, there is. I hadn't meant to say anything about this—to you or anyone else—but I guess I got caught off guard and showed what I really feel about him. He seems to think that he is more spiritual than anyone else, and some people believe him. A few of the wives treat him like a spiritual director, and he teaches them how to meditate. I don't know too much about it, but it doesn't seem to me to have much to do with Jesus. And it's hard for somebody who has been in Vietnam to be dumped on by a prissy creep like him who pretends to be so superior. He wouldn't last five minutes on a patrol."

"I see. I didn't mean to pry into your personal affairs. But if you ever want to talk about this anymore or about anything else, either I or any other member of the faculty would be available. Don't hesitate to call on us."

"Thank you, sir. I imagine it'll all blow over, but I do appreciate the offer. Well, I better get going. I've got some theology to read before Evensong. Thanks again for the help."

Bothwell sat Buddha-wise on one of the gym mats, managing to maintain his dignity unabated in these ungraceful circumstances. In spite of the aroma of ancient sweat, stale air, and liniment that proclaimed the normal function of the large basement room in the Green Building, the bachelor students had managed to create a festive air by the greenery they had draped around. Epiphany was a big day at the Clergy Training College. Since most students were home for the holidays when Christmas occurred, and strict adherence to the liturgical seasons kept the seminary from doing anything so Protestant as to have a Christmas party in Advent, January 6 was the great annual feast of the Incarnation. It was also when the single students went all out to repay the married ones for their hospitality throughout the year. First, there was a party for the children after school, with a tree and small presents. The Dean kept volunteering to don a cope and beard and appear as St. Nicholas a month overdue, but the bachelors always put him off; and Caspar, Melchior, and Balthazar would appear year after year, slightly Hoosier in their accents despite their journey from the Eastern mountains. Then some of the single students served turkey dinner to the married couples and faculty in the refectory, while others were in the Hutches sitting with the kids who had already broken their toys from the afternoon's party.

After dinner they all trooped downstairs to see what new costumes the ingenuity of the bachelors had been able to devise, along with the new talent from this year's Juniors. Once everyone had been served wassail and taken what seating was available, they sang carols, the selections limited to the more esoteric ones in the hymnal, the ones not rendered unbearable by constant repetition from radio and public speaker systems since Thanksgiving. Then the entertainment began. It started off slowly and did not build momentum until Pete Whiston began to play the fiddle. A music major from Bloomington who had almost "fried his brain" with acid when he was exploring what an electronic violin could contribute to rock, Whiston had been converted while listening to a Salvation Army band a few Christmases before. He then lived in a commune of charismatic Christians who were better at spouting Bible verses than helping the earth bring forth its increase. No one knew what had drawn him to an Episcopal seminary, but they all knew Whiston played the fiddle like someone possessed by spirits. Clean-shaven with large blue eyes that seemed focused on a distant object, Pete had a face surprisingly unlined by all he had been through. His hair was blonde and fine as corn silk, and he combed it back totally straight, only to have it flop across his face during his ecstatic translation of the music of the spheres into bluegrass abandon.

Pete was followed by John Strong, dressed as most of his classmates in jeans and carrying a Martin guitar aged to perfection. In his granny glasses and drooping moustache, Strong looked like what he was, one of the most committed anti-war activists on campus. What was not so obvious was that he had one of the best minds that had appeared on campus for years. To-night he was there to imitate Woody's boy by doing all nineteen minutes of "Alice's Restaurant." Bothwell had not heard the piece before and found it very amusing, but noticing Seth across the room, he realized that his amusement was not shared by everyone. Seth had a frown on his face, and although visibly attempting to exercise self-control, his feet tapped impatiently, while he constantly shifted positions.

The final entertainer of the evening was Sebastian Seymour. He had traded his poncho for a close-fitting embroidered gauze shirt that gave him more freedom of bodily movement. The need for this freedom became quickly apparent when he began his act, one of mime mimicry. Without saying a word and only by subtle alteration of posture and gait, he could conjure up the image of other members of the community. A few self-important strides informed everyone that he was doing the Dean. Next Dr. Jethro, the bearded Old Testament professor the students called Yahweh, was evoked with little effort. There was great wit in the caricatures, but Bothwell also recognized an element of malice. When he himself was next to be imitated, however, he was too charmed by seeing himself as others saw him to take any offence. For his last impersonation, Seymour seemed to grow taller. His delicate frame became robust, and he slung out newly long legs in a woodsman's stride. The stride became close order drill and the drill a goosestep. Sheila Clarke's gleeful laughter sounded shrill in the heavy air. Her amusement went unshared as the cavorting figure suddenly was carrying an insubstantial rifle. The figure stalked with stealth and attacked with energy. Bothwell felt he was seeing not only the bayonet, but also the bodies of unarmed civilians into which it was plunged.

# 3

The ten o'clock news had begun, recounting the latest statistics on American troops withdrawn from Vietnam, Biafrans starved, and PLO members who had come into Israel from Lebanon. The Chinese and the Russians were accusing one another of preparing for war. France had agreed to help stop the manufacture of heroin in Marseilles. There was still no real lead about who had murdered Yablonski and his wife and daughter.

All these alarms and excursions were enough to rouse Seth from his uneasy sleep in the armchair in front of the set. He had sat down after coming in from Evensong and discovering another note from Sheila. She would be late, it said. Even though a TV dinner had been left with instructions for its preparation, he decided to have a drink and look at the news, hoping she would return in time to eat with him. But after he had finished the second drink, and she still was gone, he was too agitated to eat. He thought he could study. He knew he wasn't up to attempting Braudel's French nor to following Tillich's arguments, but he could make a stab at finding out what Raymond Brown had to say about John's gospel. The print proved so tiny and the book so thick that he wondered if he could ever finish all of it, or why anyone might want to. Every car door's slam, every footstep on the sidewalk, every creak of the old Army building was enough to get him off his feet and peering out the window into the empty darkness outside.

Unable to focus on the page, he finally turned on the tube. In Vietnam, especially while in prison, he believed there was no greater luxury on earth than sitting in a comfortable living room with one's family after a hard day's work and watching television. Arriving home only in time to enter seminary in the fall, his study needs crowded out this delayed gratification. Now, like other aspects of his life, the television experience was failing to measure up to anticipation. Finally, the warmth of the room, the effect of the bourbon, and the banality of what he was watching caused him to doze off into an agitated sleep.

Just as he was rousing himself, he heard the doorknob turn and saw Sheila coming in on tiptoe. Switching on the table light he had turned off when he had abandoned his study plans, he looked up at her. "Where have you been? I worried about you."

"You look like you've been worried, boozing again and passed out in front of the TV," she said, removing her tam and scarf and hanging her coat in the closet. "Fine seminarian you make."

"I only had two, and I was not passed out, just asleep." He arose and moved toward her. "I still want to know where you've been."

"I told you in the note. I went to make my meditation."

"And it took you five hours. I knew you were getting very holy, but I didn't know that like Paul you had been 'rapt up to the third heaven.'"

"Why do you always have to put down anything that you don't understand? You know that I've been receiving instruction in meditative technique from Sebastian. We were talking about it afterwards. He says that I am making phenomenal progress." Her face tilted up, her blue eyes glistening and looking into space. With the blue highlights gleaming in her black hair, she looked as beautiful as she had when she was crowned at the state fair competition.

"What does that creep know about it?"

"You're jealous. All you husbands are. You can't stand the idea that there is one student here who is going to be a real spiritual leader. I don't know why he is here; he already knows more about spirituality than any of the faculty. He hasn't merely studied Christian asceticism—he is deep into the meditative techniques used by ancient cultures all over the world. He has advanced beyond the petty confines of Christianity into the real spirituality that lies behind all religions." She stalked into the bathroom and slammed the door behind her.

Seth continued to talk through the door. "You know what the other students call him? 'The Little Bastian.' Nobody can stand him. Even those peaceniks hate him, and they are supposed to love everybody. If you want to know my opinion, the guy is crazy. And probably queer as well. Did you ever notice the way that he walks?"

Emerging from the lighted bathroom into the unlit bedroom, Sheila stood framed in the doorway. Her model's stance with pelvis thrust forward was backlit, and the shortie nightgown she wore hardly hid her shape. There could be no doubt why she had won swimsuit at national.

"I'm glad one of the men around here is not carnal. The rest of you are a bunch of animals. All of you look at me as if I were naked. Sebastian says that sex is disruptive of the spiritual life."

With this she went to the bed, pulled back the covers, climbed onto her side, and, facing the edge, she pulled the covers around her neck. "I have to work tomorrow, so I can't lose sleep by arguing with you all night. Please don't read in bed—it keeps me awake. Goodnight."

The next morning between classes Canon Bothwell stopped in the office and told the Dean's secretary that he would like to examine the folder of one of the Juniors, Sebastian Seymour. Unlocking the file cabinet and removing a folder, she said, "Here's Mr. Seymour's file. You will find it all here except the psychological, Dr. Bothwell. The Diocese requires us to return that as soon as the Dean has read it."

"I understand, Mrs. Simmes. I'm sure the time will come when the law is much stricter about student files in every way. I only look at one when I have a real need to know something about the student. May I sit at this table while I look through this?"

Sorting through the documents, Bothwell saw that Sebastian was older than he thought, having spent about five years between his graduation from Butler and his arrival at the seminary. He had grown up in the Indiana town of Lebanon, in a working-class family, discovering a larger world in high school, where he was active in dramatics and debate and had been a cheerleader. He had attended Butler on a scholarship, and his grades there had been fairly good. His Graduate Record Exam score was higher than Bothwell had expected. His main activities were in theatre, but he was also active in a campus group sponsored by a church in the ghetto. That congregation was connected with a mainline denomination but was almost completely identified with its intense pastor, Bob Smith. Bothwell knew Smith himself had grown up in Indianapolis' inner city in one of its poor white sections, and he completed college and seminary by taking jobs on the night shift and finding every scholarship available for ministerial students. Smith's combination of ecstatic experience with social action was not typical of the denomination with which his congregation maintained a tenuous identification, and from which it received a good bit of financial aid.

Smith's church had carried on an aggressive recruitment program on the campus, looking especially for the excluded and the alienated among the student body. The combination of tongue speaking and association with blacks was enough to give a sense that, even though one was excluded from the social life on campus, those who belonged to the fraternities and sororities were the ones who were really left out. This group offered a natural sphere in which Seymour could develop his flair for leadership, and by the time he graduated he had established himself as Smith's right-hand man. After several years something must have happened to sour the relationship, because Sebastian had dissociated himself from the congregation. He set himself up in the neighborhood as an unofficial social work agent, and after a few months had started to attend the small Episcopal mission nearby. Smith had returned the seminary's reference form with a scrawl across it that said, "If he had been one of us, he would not have gone out from us. We turn him over to Satan."

Sebastian had soon made himself invaluable to St. Cyprian's mission. He became choir director and, having mastered the liturgy in a few months, a lay reader and director of acolytes. In January he was elected to the Mission Council, and by spring he was recommended as a postulant. All this information was from his autobiographical statement and references from members of the congregation. The documents also revealed that he had been approved over the opposition of the Rector of All Saints, from whose parish most of the social agencies in the Diocese operated, and who was the Episcopalian with the most credibility among the city's blacks.

After his eleven o'clock class Canon Bothwell was descending the steps in front of the School when he heard a pleasant feminine voice call, "Rod, wait up, and I'll let you walk a lady home." Turning around, he saw with satisfaction that he had been hailed by Chase's newest and only female faculty member, Angela Price-Mansfield. Her being hired surprised everyone, but from the entire group of candidates she was the best qualified in quite a strong field. Her dissertation at Duke showing the superficiality of Situation Ethics had been accepted for publication by Westminster without revision. Perhaps the most surprising aspect of her selection, however, was her acceptance of Chase's invitation, since she had a number of more attractive offers. But her husband Tony had been offered a job teaching Renaissance history at Wabash, and the package deal seemed to extend to the two of them more of the opportunities they were seeking, so Chase was able to hire above itself. Since the pay package at Chase was figured on the formula for clergy and included housing, while Wabash had only a few houses that it could make available to faculty at below-market rent, the Price-Mansfields lived at the seminary and were Roderick Bothwell's next-door neighbors.

"An honor and a pleasure, ma'am." Bothwell's formal gallantry was partly facetious because he had already come to have a great deal of affection and respect for his attractive young colleague; but it also came naturally to one whose youth had been spent in the South four decades before, and who had never been married.

"I don't know that I would have realized it was a lady I was waiting for, with your cloak so much like those the rest of us wear around here. I suspect, however, that it is we who have appropriated feminine fashions rather that you who have borrowed ours."

"Cloaks are the only outer garment the fashion designers have come up with that can cover the multitude of hem lines they have left us to choose among," she replied, falling in step beside him. The top of her head came only to the height of his earlobe, although Bothwell was of average height. Her face was narrow, but in profile her lightly made-up features were chiseled gracefully enough to have adorned a cameo.

"Still, they do come in handy for protecting books and papers from the weather when you don't like to carry an attaché case. From the point of view of the history of religions, I expect you're right about clerical vesture. The shaman is outside the conventional roles of male and female. Sometimes the way that is shown is for him to adopt feminine clothing."

"Speaking of the history of religions, how is the course going?" Bothwell queried. Angela, like several of the Chase faculty, had to double in brass and offer the seminary's few courses in an academic field other than her specialized area of ethics and moral theology.

"I like doing it. I had done a good bit of work in the field at Duke because anthropology offers so much evidence for the sociology of knowledge, which, as you know, is my main methodological interest. Still, something happened in class today that I found a little disturbing."

"What was that?"

"As is usual at the beginning of the semester, we were talking about assignments and appropriate topics for term papers. Sebastian Seymour wanted to do a paper about the use of hallucinogens to induce religious experience."

"I don't find that too surprising in the light of the interest of young people today in drugs."

"No, that's not the point of my concern. I made some of the obvious bibliographical suggestions: Castaneda and Meyerhoff's book on the peyote cult, that sort of thing. But he said that he wasn't interested in merely reading a lot of books. He wanted to move the whole issue to a much more scientific basis with controlled experiments. Apparently he subscribes to that new journal that Timothy Leary has started and was hoping to do something that could be published there."

"I see. That certainly should be discouraged."

"Yes. I'm afraid I sounded very much like an ethicist and talked about the morality of experiments on human beings using substances the impact of which we know so little. I know that LSD in light doses is not supposed to do any permanent psychological damage to emotionally healthy people, but we don't always know how stable someone is. I've seen people on bad trips, and I wouldn't wish that on anybody. And we don't really know about chromosome damage. Not to mention the legal issue."

"Yes, I can imagine the Dean's reaction if he thought it might get into the papers that seminarians were using drugs. And, as pleasant as it is to contemplate his apoplexy, I would have grave concerns myself over the effect on the students. Nor would it be to our advantage to offend those who support us financially."

Angela continued, "To make matters worse, it wasn't other students Sebastian was thinking of experimenting on. I had the distinct impression that he had in mind using some of the student wives who have accepted him as a spiritual director. And I don't think that I am the only one who got that impression. Some of the students began to look grim, especially those whose wives could be involved. Our Mr. Seymour could be playing with fire. I would not want someone like Seth Clarke, for instance, to have it in for me. How many ways do they say Green Berets are taught to kill with their bare hands? Thirty-one?" Bothwell had no answer, and they walked on in reflective silence.

By this time they had walked beyond the block of the seminary's public buildings and into the next block devoted to faculty housing. Pleasant frame dwellings representing the architectural styles of Indiana farm houses in the late-nineteenth and early-twentieth centuries faced to the inside of the block so that they shared a long open court instead of having separate lawns between them and a street. The block was enclosed on the south by the Charles Addams deanery, which faced the chapel across a long mall. Coming to her sidewalk, Angela turned to Bothwell and said in parting, "I've got to fix myself a sandwich, and I'm sure that Katrina has something scrumptious for you."

# 4

When Katrina showed Fred Andrews into Canon Bothwell's study on Friday afternoon, the professor was seated at his rolltop desk writing out a book review in his neat italic hand. He rose to welcome the senior sacristan, leaving on his desk the latest scholar's injudicious conclusions about the Elizabethan Settlement and his own listing of them.

"Come in, Fred, come in, and have a seat. How is the busiest man on campus? I've always said that one of the nicest things about serving on a seminary faculty is that you don't have to know how to do anything liturgically. Sacristans treat clergy like appliances that have only to be plugged in for performing their part. It's very spoiling. Last summer I took Sunday duty at Danville so the rector could go on vacation, and I had to find all the lessons myself. I really felt quite lost. You do a fine job of training."

"Thank you, Father. I'd feel more flattered if all of this weren't coming from the man who teaches us liturgics." He sat down on the wingtip chair in which Seth had sat a few days earlier. "And that brings me to what I needed to see you about. It's time for me to recommend someone for you to nominate to the Dean as Junior sacristan. He needs to know the ropes well enough for me to retire after Easter and get a little studying in before graduation. I'll tell you, GOE's hit me so hard that I wish the new guy had already taken over. I'd like to go away somewhere and have a nice quiet nervous breakdown."

"Now, Fred, don't tell me they were that bad. You know I'm on the General Board of Examining Chaplains and helped write the exams, so I know what was on them. And let me tell you, this new system of standardized national pre-ordination examinations is much fairer than the old system by which each man was given canonicals in his own diocese. While most of the examining chaplains did keep up in the fields they examined in and were fair in what they expected, there were always a few dioceses that treated canonicals as a form of pre-ordination hazing. Some also made them an orthodoxy check according to their own highly personalized standards of true faith. But let's get away from unpleasant subjects. Which of the Juniors do you recommend?"

"Father, it's difficult. I know who is running hardest for it—Cyril Johnson. He's something of a sacristy rat and confidently expects to be made bishop some day because he already knows all of the ceremonial for bishops—when to take off a miter and when to put it on, and whether it should be precious or plain."

"Does he? Then I'm sure that puts him several steps ahead of the bishop of this diocese. All this bishop knows is how to be a faithful pastor, a sound administrator, and a teacher of God's people. Too bad he is not really qualified."

Fred smiled at Bothwell's irony and continued, "While Cyril is very fond of all the church's millinery, I'm afraid that he doesn't have the dependability and practicality that make a good sacristan. The job is not really all that aesthetic. It mainly consists in seeing that a dozen petty details are taken care of so a service can go smoothly. If it were simply a matter of dependability, I'd recommend Seth Clarke."

"That would be an interesting sight, wouldn't it—a Green Beret laying out vestments."

"He's always done a careful job when assigned, but I guess it does take a little flair to be a good sacristan, and, for all his other abilities, liturgy is not his bag. Oddly enough, it's not Sebastian Seymour's either. He's fussy enough for it, but it's too corporate and too tame for him. He prefers something exotic in which he can be the star. Would you believe, I have gone into the chapel a couple of times around midnight to make sure that everything was ready for the next day, and I have found him there in the dark going through strange gyrations in front of the altar."

"Nothing that would constitute sacrilege, I hope."

"No, nothing like that. Just bobbing around. I guess he would call it meditative positions. Mainly I've seen him in a deep bow, weaving a little from side to side. But, to get back to the subject, I believe Harvey Stanford would do the best job. He is not outstanding, but he would be competent."

"On the basis of what I have seen of him, you're probably right. I'm happy to concur in your nomination. Is there anything else I should know as faculty consultant to the sacristans?"

"Can't think of anything. Everything is normal. We could use either a few more purificators or else some extra people to iron the ones we have.

The whole-wheat hosts are generally preferred by the community to the old 'fish food' kind. Someday we are going to have to do something about the sanctuary lamp. It comes down more easily for its weekly change of candle than it goes back up. Nothing we've tried has worked to remove the candle wax from Dr. Jethro's alb, and so that may have to be replaced. As I said, everything's pretty normal."

Later that evening Bothwell turned off the projector and rose to reach switches for the table lamps. "I hope you see now, Tony, why my interest in Unidentified Flying Objects is not merely something to fill the lonely hours of an aging bachelor. I consider my investigations to be part of my rule of life as a historian. While it has been said that a historian should believe a hundred impossible things before breakfast, it is equally important that he should doubt a thousand probable ones during the day."

Tony replied, "Your slides made the point. If we have as many recent and reliable sightings as we do with so many trustworthy witnesses and such technical resources for checking into the events, but still have so little certainty over whether we're actually receiving visitors from other planets or not, how much more skeptical ought we to be over what can be known about one individual in Florence in the sixteenth century or Avignon in the fourteenth, concerning whom we have very little documentary evidence. Knowing what the majority of his contemporaries may have been like does not necessarily tell us anything about that one individual. As you are so fond of saying, probability does not apply to historical reconstruction."

Angela stood up and stretched. "I don't know how you men can be so erudite after Katrina has stuffed us full of seafood gumbo, and we've benefitted so elegantly from Rod's wine collection. Besides, Rod, you don't know what it means to young scholars setting up housekeeping to sit in really comfortable chairs. We had nothing at Duke worth moving, and what we've been able to accumulate locally has been mostly acquired at the auction barn in Crawfordsville on Tuesday nights."

"Enough of that 'just an ignorant housewife' routine, woman," Tony said to his wife. "You know that you're the only hard-nosed intellectual among us. You read philosophers not just because you want to know who taught what when, but because you really think they might have some clue to the nature of reality. But you seem a little distracted this evening, and I know it's not because we've been talking over your head. Is something on your mind?"

"Yes," she replied. "I can't get the evening's news off my mind. I don't think I'm naive about Americans, and I've been opposed to our involvement in Vietnam since we first began sending so many advisors over during the Kennedy administration. But I was unprepared for this business at My Lai. I know information has been coming out since mid-November, but now two more soldiers have been charged with the murder of unarmed women, children, and old people. It just makes me sick. How did we ever get into a situation where something like this could happen?"

Tony nodded agreement while polishing his gold-rimmed glasses. "Yeah, it certainly makes that business with the Green Berets seem tame. Until a few months ago that was the nearest thing to an American atrocity story to have come out of the war—other than the fact that we are in it. There eight men were charged with the execution of one person, and he was someone they thought was a double agent. What does your local hero think about all that? Have you heard him say?"

"Didn't I tell you?" Angela asked. "We had a panel discussion in moral theology class about the issues in the Chuyen death, and Seth was asked to visit the class and participate. He seems to think the Special Forces are a bunch of overgrown Eagle Scouts. He told about the schools they had built in the jungle villages, and how their medics gave the natives the best health care they ever had, including some skillful amateur surgery. He pointed out that the Green Berets are experts in counterinsurgency, and they view their job to be training the local people to fight their own battles rather than having Americans fight them for them. He saw the death of Chuyen as an execution of a spy, pure and simple. He did hedge a little when one of the guys pointed out to him that his local freedom fighters were well-paid mercenaries, and he did not really have a comeback when someone said that since the Green Berets had Chuyen in custody, they were no longer in danger from him and could have allowed him to stand trial. But he seemed to have no doubt of the essential rightness of what his buddies are doing. In fact, I gather that he didn't re-enlist not only because he had felt the call to the ministry, but that he was also disgusted with the rivalry between the various intelligence services and over the lack of support the people back home were giving to heroic men who were going through hell for them."

"But, Rod," Tony said, "We still haven't answered Angela's original question. How did a clean-living country like ours get involved in a war like this? Are the revisionists right in saying that ever since World War II we have been involved in capitalistic expansion in Europe, and that our imperialism has forced Russia to take defensive measures which we then have called aggression?"

"That's not the kind of question I want to be involved in with a younger colleague. I'm sure all you young Turks in grad schools have kept far better abreast of such discussions than I have. But I do have some thoughts on the subject."

"Seriously, we'd like to hear them. I'll admit I was baiting you a little, but I do want to know what you think. I've read a lot of material, but I still have unanswered questions."

"Well, Tony, the way it looks to me is that until World War II we were an isolationist country that was able to remain rather naive about international affairs. But our situation coming out of that war virtually forced us into involvement. And I do not buy the revisionist thesis. I think Russia was expansionist, and we were not. We did become involved in order to stop aggression, and I think we did so with relatively pure motives. I don't know of any historical parallel to the Marshall Plan, for instance. But we had too much too quickly. We somehow moved from supporting righteous causes to thinking a cause was righteous because we supported it. And we came to be fascinated with our skill in playing the game of international diplomacy. Angela, I've not really checked out all the connections historically, and you would know far better than I do, but I've always thought that somehow Reinhold Niebuhr got involved in all of this."

"What do you mean?"

"Niebuhr said that we cannot allow ourselves the luxury of imagining that we are uninvolved. He said in effect—I think I'm really quoting Paul Ramsey, but I consider the point of view 'Niebuhrian'—that if the Good Samaritan had come along five minutes earlier, while the attack was still going on, he would have had to decide what then would be the most loving response. Should he protect the man who had fallen among thieves, or should he refuse to involve himself in violence even if it meant that the man who was being attacked might die? Would he not decide in fact who would die? By intervening he could see that it was the robber rather than the robbed that died, while by standing aloof he would guarantee that it would be the innocent who suffered. I wonder if such thinking did not get us to a position very near to saying that the end justified the means? That seems to be what young Clarke is saying.

"I also think we developed a fascination with gadgetry as much as we did with power. The admiration of John Kennedy and John Foster Dulles for James Bond is a case in point. They bought into the myth of espionage as Fleming fantasized about it. Don't forget that John le Carré and other authors were writing about the kinds of duplicity with one's own people that so-called civilized nations resorted to. The final ingredient was a naive young nation just off the farm getting involved with the mysterious East where corruption was no longer in its infancy. This is what I think."

Angela, who had been wrinkling her brow during the last part of the Canon's remarks, said, "You're on to something, Rod. What seems especially ironic is that some who are the most strenuously opposed to the violence in Vietnam on moral grounds are the very ones who have started bombing buildings here in protest of the war. That movement is going to spread, I'm afraid. But this means that even for the Weathermen the issue is not whether the use of violence is ever justified, but rather what are the causes for which it may legitimately be used. We have all drunk from the same cup of violence."

At this point Tony stood up. "Lots to think about. I won't reply because I want to think about what you have said. Also, we need to be getting home to bed. Come on, Angela. Saturday is a work day at Wabash."

Helping them with their coats, Bothwell donned his own as well. "I need to go to the library to check one so-called fact in the book I'm reviewing so I can give the review to Mrs. Strong in the morning to type. Since she has a full-time job, weekends contain the only time she can spare for a middle-aged scholar who never learned to type."

"As Pogo would say, Rod," Angela said, presenting a cheek to be kissed goodnight, "'mechanical spelling do have its hazards.' Thank Katrina for us. It was a scrumptious dinner. And the conversation and company weren't bad either."

Walking down the close to the library, Roderick Bothwell was gratified to note the crispness of the air. They might get their first snow before morning. The lights along the sidewalks gave an idyllic appearance to the whole campus. In this tranquil setting, how far away all violence seemed. Bothwell was too experienced in the life of religious communities to imagine that living in one was to escape the conflicts of the world. No, a community such as a seminary, monastery, or convent was not a school for charity because all who lived in it were nice. Rather, it was precisely because people in such communities were anything but sweet and gentle that they had to find creative ways of living together. Here in a controlled environment one could encounter the abrasiveness of other personalities head on and hope that something good would come of it. But he knew too well such happy outcomes were by no means inevitable.

Climbing up the steps into the School and entering through its low, wide, rounded fortress door, he was surprised by—and surprised—a young man stealthily emerging from the library. Although he did not get a good look at the face, Bothwell experienced a vague sense of recognition. This was not a student, or he would have certainly known him. And no seminarian would have dressed in a nice conservative suit and topcoat, not even on a Friday night. Bothwell dismissed the identity of the man as none of his business. Turning into the library, he was not surprised to see the lights still burning brightly at midnight on the first Friday night of the term. Some of the older students, long removed from academic settings, found the going rough and had to set a steady pace for themselves at the beginning of the semester if they hoped to arrive successfully at the end.

Beyond the circulation desk on the right of the entrance and the card catalog on the left, the reading room was furnished with long oak tables, the bookracks down their centers serving the students on both sides. The table-tops sloped from these centers; their golden-varnished surfaces reflecting glare from the long, low-hanging light fixtures. A spiral iron staircase in the back right-hand corner led to stacks on the floor above and in the basement beneath.

The only one burning the midnight oil turned out to be Steve Wilson, who had managed the Singer sewing machine outlet in a county seat in downstate Illinois before deciding that God was calling him to the priesthood, and therefore—although he was not sure he saw the connection—to seminary. Wilson stood up when he saw his professor entering, which revealed he was wearing narrow-legged olive green slacks, a bright yellow dress shirt, and a vivid plaid tie that the Canon could only consider regrettable. How nice that Wilson would be in clericals in a couple of years, and that such sartorial excesses would be curbed. Yet he would probably want to wear those new clergy shirts being put out in a rainbow of loud colors.

"Good evening, Mr. Wilson. Your zeal is commendable, but I imagine it makes for a bleak weekend for Mrs. Wilson. Do you really need to study so late?"

"I do, Doc. Being a business major did not prepare me for this kind of work. To tell the truth, I never was much of a student. It is rough on Sherry, but I keep thinking how much rougher it would be on her if I didn't do it.

She is sacrificing so much for me to be here that I can't let her down by flunking out. But for the last hour I might as well have not been here."

"Oh, why is that?"

"It's Seth Clarke. You may not know, but he's been my best buddy here. We're not like these young kids just out of college. The work comes harder for us, and we don't see things the same way they do. I've been worried about Seth for some time. I hope I'm not telling tales out of school, but things haven't been going well between him and Sheila."

To ease Wilson's discomfort, Bothwell said, "I gathered as much."

"Oh, you knew? We aren't sure exactly how much the faculty knows about what goes on down in the Hutches. Sheila has been going to Sebastian Seymour for lessons in meditation and spiritual counsel, and it's really been burning Seth up. Tonight he ate in the refectory because he was afraid if he went home he'd find another note and TV dinner. He stayed up here studying with me until 10:30, but he was mighty restless. Finally he went home."

"I'm sure in the circumstances that was the right thing to do."

"Yeah, but he didn't stay. He was back in fifteen minutes and whiter than a sheet. I've never seen anybody so mad. This time the note didn't say that she was out only for the evening. It said that she'd taken the car and gone out of town on a private retreat. The first night she will be alone purifying her thoughts, but tomorrow Sebastian will come, and he promised to initiate her into a new plateau of spirituality. Seth thought Sebastian was going to try to get her hooked on some kind of dope he's been experimenting with, maybe acid. Seth was looking for him. Said he was going to kill the son of a bitch. You know, Doc, I better go look for the guy before he gets in trouble. Sebastian isn't worth Seth's messing up his life."

"You're right, Mr. Wilson. If I can be of any help, don't hesitate to call on me, whatever the time of day or night. I agree that this could be a very nasty situation, and Mr. Clarke is too fine a young man to be wasted."

After Wilson left, the Canon felt too upset to concentrate on his study. He kept wondering what he should or could do. He did, however, succeed in checking his reference. He had been right; the author had suppressed the evidence that was inconsistent with his thesis. Bothwell turned out the library lights and went outside. As he started for home, snow began to fall.

# 5

Almost four inches of snow had fallen by the time Fred Andrews walked out of the Green Building the next morning. The front had moved on, leaving the cloudless sky a bright blue and the temperature twenty degrees colder than the night before. The world looked new made. As he walked over to the chapel to make whatever last-minute arrangements might be necessary for Morning Prayer and Eucharist at 7:30, Fred noticed that no fresh footprints disturbed the new snow. It did appear that while the snow was falling someone had walked into the chapel from the Green Building, and someone had walked out of it and down the walk in front of the School, heading in the direction of faculty houses and the Hutches, but these prints had been filled in by later snow, and now were little more than indentations, pockmarks in the white face of the earth.

Opening the double door, he turned on the narthex light and went through the swinging door into the chapel itself. The morning light slanted brilliantly onto the floor through the high, round-topped Georgian windows so that motes of dust could be seen dancing in the broad beams of sunshine. As he walked through the court of the gentiles and past the faculty stalls, he saw what looked like a pile of sheets on the floor in front of the Dean's stall. Looking more closely, he saw that the mound of cloth was in fact Sebastian's poncho and madras pants. Has the guy gone to sleep while making his meditation, Fred wondered. Maybe he was coming down off something and had passed out. That's all we need, a drugged-out seminarian! Stooping, Fred leaned over to smell Seymour's breath. There was no odor, nor any evidence of breathing. He peeled back an eyelid. The eye underneath did not move. Jumping to his feet, Fred ran back to the sacristy and dialed Canon Bothwell's number on the campus phone system.

"Father, you had better come quick. Sebastian Seymour is lying on the floor of the chapel, and I think he's dead. What should I do? Should I call the Dean?"

"No, Fred, I'll be right there. No need to worry the Dean until we know what to worry him about. Stand in front, and don't let anyone in. If the Middler sacristan comes, tell him to go into the sacristy by the outside door so that he can take the vessels and vestments over to the library, and we can have the liturgy there. Meanwhile just tell people that an emergency has come up, and it's being attended to."

When Bothwell arrived at the chapel, he left Fred outside to direct worshipers to the library while he tried to ascertain whether Sebastian was dead. Getting down on his knees, he placed an ear in the middle of Seymour's back. He was not surprised when he heard nothing, because the poncho was thick and, besides, he thought it likely that a heartbeat could be heard only from in front. In case the boy was dead, and an investigation needed to be made, he did not turn over the body. Instead, he took from his pocket a small hand mirror he'd located before leaving home and placed it in front of Sebastian's nose and mouth. When the mirror remained unfrosted, he picked up the young man's outstretched hand and pressed the nail of the index finger with his thumb. Seeing no flushing under the nail when he released the pressure, he got up and walked to the telephone in the sacristy. First he called Myron Evans, a physician whose office was in Crawfordsville, but whose residence on a farm about halfway into town from the seminary made him a convenient medical man for Chase to have on retainer. Then he called the sheriff's office and informed the switchboard operator that a student had died at the Clergy Training School under circumstances that bore investigation.

Going through the swinging doors into the narthex, he was met by a sputtering Dean coming through the double doors over the protest of the Senior sacristan. Even in his present agitated state, it was obvious that The Very Reverend J. Stanley Huston was an extraordinarily handsome man. At least three inches over six feet tall, his blond hair stood in dramatic contrast to dark, long-lashed cocker spaniel eyes. His regular features reminded Bothwell of the sketched profiles of the young men in Arrow shirt ads he'd seen in his youth. Although crow's-feet had begun to appear by his eyes, small red capillaries could be seen in his cheeks, and his jawline had lost some of its boney clarity, he still bore a distinction worth thousands of dollars a year to the seminary's fund-raising efforts.

At the moment the most perfect liturgical voice in Bothwell's memory had lost some of its resonance. "Roddy, what's all this about? A student's trying to keep me out of my own chapel! Did he say that a Junior has been injured? Why wasn't I notified? Why did I have to learn about it at the chapel door like everyone else?"

"Mr. Andrews reported his discovery to me because I am the faculty member with whom he ordinarily consults. I did not inform you because I don't like to disturb you until I have a full report to make. You are too busy to be bothered by guesses and speculations. Yes, one of the Juniors, Mr. Seymour, is lying on the chapel floor and gives no indication of life. I called Dr. Evans immediately and, since there is nothing around that suggests how death may have occurred, I also called the sheriff."

"Why did you have to go and do that, Bothwell?" the Dean exploded. "Nobody seems to appreciate the trouble I go to around here to keep this place going. Something like this is bound to get into the papers, and it could undo years of work in building up the reputation of the seminary as the sort of place that substantial people should support. Do you think it's too late to call back and tell them not to come?"

"No, I'm afraid not. And besides, Mr. Dean, do you think it would be wise? The only thing I know that would frighten off prospective donors more than the investigation of a crime on campus would be the impression that we had something to hide and were trying to cover up. I'm sure the sheriff's investigation will prove that the seminary has no complicity in unsavory events. Our best protection is to make every effort to get to the bottom of this unfortunate occurrence as soon as possible."

"I suppose you're right," the Dean said, taking on the aspect of a dutiful citizen. "I will meet the sheriff and assure him of our full cooperation. As the Attorney General pointed out—and as Vice President Agnew has also said—it will take the full effort of the better element of the country to restore law and order in these days of crime in the streets. Besides, maybe the Sheriff will listen to reason about not informing the press before we have any evidence that a crime has been committed."

A two-toned brown sedan with a gold shield on the door and a row of lights across the top approached the town of New Charleston, its tires bumping on the ridges of tar between the concrete sections of the snowplowed and pitted highway. The town looked much as it had one hundred thirty years earlier when Bishop Chase had arrived there, searching for a place to start over after his disappointment in the intractability of the faculties of Kenyon and Bexley Hall. He thought he had found a good thing near Crawfordsville. With Wabash College there he would not have to create a college department to give his prospective students the preliminary grounding so badly needed by young frontiersmen who wished to study for holy orders. But it was best not to be too close to the Presbyterians, so he went down Sugar Creek about ten miles to this community, recently founded by good Episcopalians from South Carolina who had sojourned in Ohio for a generation before moving out west to Montgomery County.

The town now looked as it had then, except for the paved highway, telephone poles, and TV antennas. Its population had hovered around four hundred for nearly a century and a half. Most of its buildings were deployed along the highway, which stretched towards Yountsville in the east and Alamo in the west. It was seldom more than two blocks deep on either side of the highway, except at the right turn the road took in the very center of town. At that corner were clustered two of the town's six filling stations, an IGA food store, and a half dozen other places of business. Even there so little disturbed the peace of the town's busiest intersection that at most hours of the day New Charleston's only traffic light could be distinctly heard switching from green to red and back again. The air was usually so still that one could tell some minutes afterwards that a truckload of pigs had passed on the way from the feeder lot to the market. Although large, hollow, illuminated plastic signs bore witness to the attachment of the town to a wider, more modern world, the buildings were mostly left over from an earlier era when horsepower was harnessed to a singletree, and the only people who bought bread were those who had no kitchen in which to bake their own.

The Sheriff's car, as it turned at the light, bore with ruffled dignity its allusion to a recent TV comedy series, *Car 54, Where Are You?* Indiana was divided into districts with designating numbers that appeared on area license plates and was painted on tops of local law enforcement vehicles in letters large enough to be recognized from the air. Montgomery County was area 54, and thus sheriff Wade Bryant rode under that blazon as he came to the western edge of New Charleston and turned north along the side of the four square blocks of the campus of Chase Clergy Training College. The school had its back to the highway, trying to look as if it were in the world, but not of it. That impression was strengthened by the lack of anything but cow pastures between the campus and the woods.

It was only as they drove along the snow-covered campus that Bryant turned his attention to the task ahead and discussed with the young deputy beside him anything more related to their profession than high school basketball, an annual fever achieving epidemic proportions in Indiana. "You know, Horace, as many times as I have been by this place, I don't think I've ever been inside. You belong to their church, don't you? Do you know anything about what goes on here?"

"Yeah, Wade. I've been coming to things out here since I was a kid, and for a while at the end of high school, and when I was first at Bloomington, I thought I would be studying here, but then I decided that I didn't have the call. I do know one member of the faculty pretty well. Canon Bothwell has been helping out at St. John's in Crawfordsville on Sundays as long as I can remember, and he's always been kinda my advisor. He's the Sub-dean here. That means he's the number-two man."

"Well, that contact ought to help," the sheriff said as they pulled into the visitor's parking lot behind the chapel. "I don't know what they mean by 'death in circumstances that bear investigation.' I guess somebody could have killed somebody in a place like this. I've seen stranger things in thirty years of law enforcement. Do you think they'll want to hush it up and interfere with our investigation?"

Getting out of the car, the young deputy stretched his athletic frame, buttoned his dark brown uniform parka, and put on his western-styled felt hat with the shield on front and its acorn-ended brown cord band. "I know Canon Bothwell won't. He's an historian and just as anxious to get the facts as Joe Friday on *Dragnet*. Don't know about the Dean. I haven't seen much of him, but I get the impression he likes things to be seen in the most favorable light."

The sheriff, emerging from the car and also stretching, stood taller than his assistant and just as straight. "Well, whatever it is, we're going to have to get to the bottom of it, whether they like it or not. Let's go."

Walking across the fresh snow, they went down the side of the chapel, its red bricks gleaming in the morning sun. Coming through the arcade, they saw Canon Bothwell and the Dean standing on the steps and talking to the doctor. Myron Evans, overcoat collar turned up and gloved hands grasping his medical bag, turned toward them and said by way of greeting, "Wade, it looks like you've got a corpse on your hands. I'm sorry I had to disturb the scene of death, but we did know that we had someone who might be helped by a doctor, and we don't know that a crime has been committed. I'd guess he's been dead about six to eight hours. The body temperature has gone down a little, but the chapel is heated so that doesn't tell us much. There is postmortem lividity, so we know he's been there a while and that the body hasn't been moved. Rigor mortis is just moving down below the neck, so, like I say, six to eight hours."

"Thank you, Myron. You ought to be the coroner. You'd certainly beat the undertaker we got. What did he die from?"

"Can't tell without examining the body. Since he was obviously dead, and there's nothing to show why, I thought I'd better disturb him as little as possible until you could get your investigation underway. The Dean here says that he's going to call the boy's parents over in Lebanon and tell them he's dead. Maybe you want to get on the phone and also tell 'em we're going to do an autopsy. I've called the funeral home to take the body to the morgue when you're finished with it."

The sheriff sent his deputy ahead to take charge of the chapel area while he took part in the phone call. A sad business, telling folks their only child was dead and that his body would have to be cut up to find out why. Arriving at the chapel, he found that Horace had already begun to look over the body and go through the other initial steps for investigating what might be the scene of a crime. He was a good boy, solid as they come and bright without being a smart aleck. They had done a good job with him at the Law Enforcement Academy, too. The youngest of the three deputies, he was also far and away the best for something like a murder investigation. They only had two or three a year, usually over family matters, with little doubt who had done what. This one could get fancier. At least they would have no problem identifying the body. The Dean had told him a little about the boy. They might have to find out a lot more, depending on how the postmortem turned out.

"Better get your camera, Horace, and all the other gear. I have a feeling we need do this one by the book."

Two hours later the corpse had been studied, and it and the chapel had been photographed, sketched, and searched. The ambulance arrived to remove the body, and the coroner was asked to order an autopsy. As systematic as the search had been, it turned up little to contribute to an explanation of the Seymour boy's death. Nothing resembling a weapon was around, nor was there anything that could have been involved in a natural death. Since there were no open wounds on the body, there were no spots or pools of blood. The chapel had been due for its weekly cleaning later that day, and so footprints and fingerprints had been accumulating since the previous Saturday; presumably those of all the faculty and student body would be found. The ledges in front of the pews and the bookracks underneath were all examined. In addition to the books needed to participate in the services and devotional aids used by the various members of the community, they also contained such personal items as handkerchiefs, letters, cough drops, and even one comic book, but nothing that seemed to bear any relation to the death of a seminarian or to offer any explanation for it. The only item that appeared worth sealing in an envelope was a matchstick with the head broken off and the other end chewed. It had been under the body when it was removed, and on the dark stained floor it had been a tiny light spot in the middle of the anthropomorphic outline in chalk.

"Okay, Horace," the sheriff said, "That's all we can do until we hear what Doc Evans learns from the autopsy, and I hope and pray it's all we will have to do. I'd hate to have to investigate a murder at this place. It's always had a good reputation in the community. I wouldn't like to see that changed."

When the officers had finished in the chapel, word was passed, and the community gathered to say the Litany for the Dying for Sebastian, postponing a requiem until funeral plans had been made. While few had cared for him outside the coterie of women who regarded him as a spiritual guide, he was a member of the community and a Christian as well as a postulant for holy orders, and the repose of his soul was an appropriate subject for their prayers. At first the shock of a death in the community left everyone stunned, but by evening the nervousness that the sight of the death of a contemporary brings to the young was generating a lot of speculation about how Sebastian had died. No one was yet ready to mention the possibility of murder, especially by a member of the community, although local antipathies were widely known. At supper in the refectory one of the Middlers compared the investigative procedures to those in *Alice's Restaurant*, with "Eight-by-ten glossy color photographs with crosses and circles and writing on the back." Meanwhile, the Dean had flown to New York where he had been scheduled to preach on theological education at an affluent parish.

At midafternoon Sebastian's parents arrived. To Canon Bothwell they looked dazed but apparently found the death of their son (whom they had not seem since his sophomore year at Butler) no more incomprehensible than they had found the boy himself. It was obvious that any personal dreams they held on to had not focused on him for some time. Perhaps there was a vestige of a hope against hope that he would someday return and fit into the only world they understood, but it was overpowered by their amazement that a figure so exotic could have come from their loins and their home. They agreed readily to the Canon's suggestion that, when the authorities were through with their son's body, the funeral should be held from the seminary chapel, and the interment should be in the campus cemetery. A funeral from their church would have seemed out of place, and their son had little call on the grief of their neighbors; indeed, their own grieving had mainly taken place when they had begun to deal with the estrangement of a son who seemed like a changeling. They would return to Lebanon much as they had left, with only the difference that the loss of their boy was now a certainty and not just an overwhelming probability.

Horace Jones and his wife Beth had just settled down to watch the *Saturday Night Movie*, having washed and put away the supper dishes and put their three-year-old daughter and one-year-old son to bed with hopes that they would stay there quietly. When the phone rang, Horace went to the hall to answer it on the assumption they had come to make after five years' married life that a call to a lawman's house was usually for him. When he returned he was putting on his tie and walking toward his gun belt and holster. "It was Wade," he said. "He's coming by. We've got to go back out to the seminary. The student was killed by a blow on the back of the neck that broke his spinal cord. It's almost impossible to do that by falling backwards on something, so it sounds like the old blunt instrument event. Not an accident. I sure don't like the sound of it."

"Do you mean that someone at the Clergy Training College murdered him? That's awful!"

"Yeah, and I got an idea that I don't like any better than the rest of it. Those classes I take on karate in Lafayette on Wednesday nights? I'm thinking that one of the deathblows in karate is just like what happened to that seminarian. I hope we don't find anyone out there who knows karate and had it in for this guy. That could look bad." They heard the sound of a car horn being softly tapped. "Wade's here. I've got to go."

"I'll try to stay awake for you. It's Saturday night." She looked wistfully at the TV set.

"Being in law enforcement sure can interfere with the life of a married man. I'll see you when I can, honey." Kissing her hurriedly, he grabbed his hat and coat and ran out the door.

# 6

It was almost a quarter of nine before the sheriff and his deputy arrived at New Charleston, gone to the deanery, and then been directed to the door of Canon Bothwell. Katrina and her husband Frank had gone to spend the evening with their daughter's family out of town, so the door was answered by the Canon himself, who had been in his study reading the galleys of his new book. Welcoming the officers and taking their coats, he took them to his study rather than the living room because, he explained to them, "This is the kind of night when everyone likes to sit in front of a roaring fireplace." His domestic skills did extend to pouring coffee for them from the pot Katrina had left plugged in. Then, after they were comfortably situated with their cups of coffee, he said, "I don't imagine you bring good news. You wouldn't have come this far at night to tell us that we have nothing to fear. I suppose you found evidence suggesting that Mr. Seymour met his death by foul play."

"That's right, Reverend," the sheriff began. "We found that one of the boy's vertebrae had been broken and his spinal cord severed. It's almost impossible for that to happen in a fall, and we didn't see anything in the chapel that could have caused it accidentally. If the injury was inflicted by some kind of blunt object, then somebody carried it off, and the most likely person to do that would be the one that wielded it. Deputy Jones here has pointed out that karate experts know how to give that blow with their bare hands. In fact, he says it takes just ten pounds of force if applied correctly."

"Amazing that so much damage can be done with so little effort. How does that work, Horace?" the Canon asked.

"Let me qualify that a little. In karate you look at power differently from the western way. For instance, if I wanted to break this nice china cup with a karate blow—which I would never want to do, but if I did, I wouldn't think about the force of my hand at the moment of impact with the top of the cup. In fact, I wouldn't think about the cup at all. I'd think about the top of the desk where I wanted the side of my hand to end up. I'd be in a state of mind where the cup did not exist at all. So, in delivering the blow we're talking about, he wouldn't think of the neck bone, he would think of the spinal cord."

Bothwell looked intrigued. "In other circumstances it would be interesting to discuss the philosophical implications of all that, but as things are, I suppose we must restrict our curiosity to the subject at hand. You believe, Sheriff, do you, that someone at the seminary did strike such a blow on Mr. Seymour, either with some blunt object or with his hand in the manner that Deputy Jones has described?"

"That seems to sum it up, Reverend, as much as I hate to say so. I've got to ask if you know of any enemies the young man had."

"As a matter of fact, I do, Sheriff, although I cannot believe that the one I know about could have perpetrated such a crime. Indeed, he was heard to utter what may have been interpreted as a threat against Mr. Seymour at a time shortly before this terrible deed occurred. And, to make matters worse, he is the one person on campus who certainty knows karate."

"I will have to ask you his name, sir."

"He's one of our first-year students. His name is Seth Clarke. But I'm certain that he wouldn't have done such a thing."

"You don't mean Indiana's Medal of Honor winner, do you?" the sheriff asked, his eyes widening. "I'd heard he was out here, but it sure would never have occurred to me to associate him with something like this."

"Canon, I can't believe it," Horace said. "I know him a little. I used to see him at diocesan Canterbury Club meetings at Waycross, and when we were both freshmen he played end for Purdue and I was third-string quarterback for Indiana."

Bothwell told them about his conversation with Steve Wilson the night before, and what he knew of Seth's anger about Sebastian's influence over Sheila, mentioning especially the possibility that Sebastian might administer drugs to those he was directing and Sheila's plans to be away for the weekend on a retreat with him.

"I sure do hate to hear this," the sheriff said. "I was as proud of that boy as everybody in the state of Indiana. It's a pity he had to come to this."

"I don't consider it his fault," Horace added. "Boy, if somebody was trying to get Beth on dope and take her away for the weekend, I might do worse than this."

The Canon interrupted. "Aren't you in a hurry to decide that the young man is guilty? You don't have any real evidence against him so far. All you know is that he had a motive, and that he had the knowledge of how the crime could be committed. You have nothing that shows that he actually did it and, let me tell you, I do not believe for one minute that Mr. Clarke is guilty."

The sheriff made a soothing wave of his big hand. "Now, Reverend, I know you hate to think the worst of one of your students . . ."

"But that's just where you are wrong, Sheriff. I've taught here for thirty years, and during that time I've known at least two sociopaths, several alcoholics, one person who was addicted to narcotics, a number of men who had a homosexual orientation, with several of them known to be active. Three of my former students have been deposed for having sexual relations with female parishioners, two for embezzling parish funds. Several have left a string of unpaid debts behind them. For others the priesthood has been a way to rise in the world, a means of becoming the center of attention, or an escape from a world that demanded too much of them. I am as aware that my profession has not always attracted the best people as you are of the same sad state in yours. And my profession deals with sin as yours deals with crime. I cannot afford to be naive about how widespread it is. And, as a church historian, no data is so familiar to me as that of how much evil has been done by clergy. No, when I say that I do not think Mr. Clarke could have done this, I am not being sentimental, but am drawing on experience of human nature that is as acute and profound as that of a psychiatrist. Through the years I have come to trust my intuition, because it has been right so often."

"I'm sorry I misjudged you. Still, it looks bad for the boy—and I don't want him to be guilty either—but our first loyalty is to find out the truth. We do have one small clue that could point us in a different direction. I'll have to ask you to keep this completely confidential, because it's the one lead we have other than what we've discussed. Is there anyone around here who breaks the head off kitchen matches and chews the stems? We found one like that under the body. We can match up saliva from it with blood type. It's amazing how long the traces remain—sometimes over three months."

"Sheriff, you're not helping at all. The only person I know who chews matchsticks like that is Seth Clarke. He was a forestry major in college and instinctively will not leave anything around that could start a fire."

"Well, in that case we better go talk to the boy. Would you like to come with us?"

It was only a short walk from the Canon's house to the Hutches, since married student housing was on the block immediately west of the faculty housing. The three men walked out of Bothwell's back gate, crossed the street, and walked to the sidewalk between the two southernmost military apartment buildings on the campus side of the block. The sidewalk in front of 2B where the Clarkes lived had not been shoveled, and the snow was unmarred except for shallow indications, left by someone who had passed a few hours after the snow had begun falling. A rolled newspaper leaned against the step. No lights shined inside. The sheriff motioned for Horace to go around to the back and then knocked loudly. Jane Spruling, who lived in 2A with her Middler husband and their two pre-school sons, looked out her door. Recognizing the church history professor, she said, "Sheila's not there, Dr. Bothwell. She's out of town for the weekend. We did hear Seth come in at about two o'clock this morning—you know how thin the walls are—but we haven't heard a thing from him since."

After the Canon thanked her, she went back inside, and he knocked again. Several minutes passed with no response. He knocked again, this time more loudly. A muffled voice from within shouted, "Go away!" Cupping his hands to the window, he called as loudly as he could, "Seth, it's Canon Bothwell. I have two men here with me, and we need to see you about something important." A light came on back in the apartment, silhouetting a figure moving down the hall. Then the living room light came on, and the door opened. Seth stood there in rumpled plaid shirt and khakis, his boot socks bagging on his feet and his crew cut forming a rosette on the side of his head as though it had been pressed down. Blond stubble gleamed when his cheek turned to the light, and his eyes were red and puffy.

"Come in, Canon. You'll have to pardon the apartment. Sheila's out of town, and I have slept in all day."

"Seth, this is Sheriff Bryant, and we will be joined shortly by Deputy Jones. They wish to ask you some questions. Mr. Seymour has been involved in an accident, and they think you may be able to give them some information to help them in their investigation."

"That creep. It couldn't happen to a nicer guy, but I don't know anything about it."

Stamping the snow off his shoes on the mat, the sheriff came in and sat down on the sofa with Bothwell, looking across at Seth who had sat down in the recliner, rubbing his eyes and still obviously trying to get his bearings.

"Son," he said, "we need to know where you were between the time you left the library last night a little before midnight and when you came back here around two a.m."

Pulling himself into focus, Seth said cautiously, "I went from the library over to the Green Building to look for someone, but he wasn't in. I must have stood around for about five minutes trying to figure out what to do next, and then I went to the chapel. I stayed there until I came back here."

"Did you see anybody else while you were there?"

"No, sir."

By this time Horace Jones had come to the door, entered, and stood just inside. Looking up, Seth reflected puzzlement for a second and then enlightenment. "Hi, Horace, come on in. I knew you were from Crawfordsville, but I had lost track. Say, what's this all about?"

Receiving a nod of permission from the sheriff, the deputy said, "It looks bad, Seth. This fellow Seymour is dead, and shortly before it happened you told somebody you were going to kill him."

"Dead? How did that happen?"

Again receiving the nod, Horace said, "He was found in the chapel this morning with his neck broke. A blow from behind caught him between the third and fifth cervical vertebrae. From the condition of the body it looks like it happened sometime between one and three o'clock this morning."

"Oh, my God!" Seth buried his face in his hands.

"So you can see, son, why it's so important for us to know exactly what happened when you were in the chapel," the sheriff said.

"Yeah, I can see all right, but I don't know how much help I can be. I guess you know my wife was away for the weekend, and I thought she was going to meet him. I don't know if I really thought she was going to sleep with him or not; somehow he doesn't seem much like the type—or didn't, I should say. I was afraid that he might try to get her on dope. We haven't been getting along too well lately, but I love her out of my mind. The idea that he might do that to her drove me wild. If I had found him when I went to his room, I don't know what would have happened, but he wasn't there, and nobody who was up had any idea where he was—or, at least, they didn't tell me. When I couldn't find him, I just stood there feeling frustrated. I didn't know what to do about anything. After a little, though, I remembered when I was in prison in Vietnam, and things were shitty and I couldn't do anything about it, the only thing that helped was praying. So I went to the chapel. You say I was there around two hours. I don't know. I'm accustomed to putting in some pretty long stints. But he didn't come in while I was there. Nobody did."

"What did you do when you got home?" the sheriff asked.

"I guess it would be pretty obvious if you looked through the apartment so I might as well tell you, although, Canon Bothwell, I'm mighty ashamed for you to know this. For once prayer wasn't enough. I just couldn't make contact. I kept thinking about the two of them together, and Sheila under the influence of that creep and maybe getting hooked on something, and I couldn't keep my mind on my prayers. Finally I came back here, and all I wanted to do was get completely out of it. I couldn't stand my thoughts. And so I set myself down to get systematically drunk. Finally I passed out and stayed out until you woke me."

Saying this, Seth put his hand into his left shirt pocket and took out a headless match and began to chew on it thoughtfully. The Sheriff said, "I'm going to have to ask you for that match."

Seth looked startled but passed it over to him.

Standing, the sheriff said, "And get your coat, son. I'm afraid I'm going to have to take you in."

The Canon, also rising, said, "Sheriff, may I accompany you?"

"Well, Reverend, of course. But we're not going to do anymore tonight. And you can't get him out on bail on first-degree murder. We can't arraign him until the judge comes in Monday. We'll do some more questioning tomorrow. If he wants a lawyer, he could have one then. But there's not much more that can happen tonight. If you want to come, you can. Nobody's going to mistreat him."

"No, I don't expect that. I would like to be with him for awhile, to comfort him and talk with him a little, if that's all right."

# 7

The Canon returned to his house expecting to pick up his car keys and drive into town, but he discovered Katrina and Frank already home, sitting in the kitchen having a cup of coffee before retiring. When Frank heard the Canon's plans he would have none of them.

"Now, Canon," he said, "You know how to drive and have never had any accidents when you tried, but driving you is part of my job. It's easy enough for you to get studyin' about somethin' and takin' your mind off the road in ordinary times. With somethin' like this botherin' you, you'd just be worse, and I couldn't sleep knowin' you was out there on those roads in the condition they're in. We only just got in, and I can tell you that the State of Indiana ain't suddenly got better in the quality of snow plowin' it does on country roads."

Riding into town in the dark and comfort of the immense back seat, the priest was wrapped in furious thought. The analytical mind that had demolished with such skill the elaborate reconstructions of an army of ambitious historians quickly weighed the strengths and weaknesses of the case against Seth. With his own canons of evidence that were as severe as those of the law itself, he knew that there was no conclusive demonstration of any connection between the ex-soldier and the death of his fellow student, but he knew that juries could be more gullible than scholars. The process that had been initiated could end up in court not only with a capital charge against Seth, but even with a conviction and sentence. To make the situation entirely ironic, Bothwell knew too that no one in the court would really blame Seth for the crime with which they charged him. A crime that the Canon was convinced that Seth had not committed.

The 1946 Packard limousine wound around curves and up hills through lighted streets toward the courthouse square. The dark blue car, which had belonged to the Canon's mother, was the sacred commitment not only of Frank, but also of an independent garage owner in New Charleston who used his vacations to tour junkyards looking for replacement parts. Frank edged it into a parking place between two empty ones, wanting no one to splash slush onto its gleaming finish or spotless white sidewalls. Getting out, Bothwell noticed absently that they were parked in front of what he and his high school friends had always referred to as a "monument to Southern marksmanship," sublimely heedless of the fact that statues honoring Civil War dead decorated an even higher percentage of courthouse lawns in the South than they did in the North.

The classic revival building was in darkness except for a naked bulb under an enamel shade illuminating the steps down into the basement entrance and a small black glass sign with its bakelite-like surface whitely interrupted by the legend of POLICE through which twinkled the glow of a low-wattage bulb. Entering, the Canon found a dispatcher on duty at the switchboard behind the counter. Removing his earphones and rising from his chair, the officer selected a key from the large ring on his belt and moved toward the barred door of the elevator. "Go on up, Reverend. They're expecting you. We don't book 'em and print 'em anymore since that Miranda decision, so the sheriff and Horace have already gone home. The jailer knows you're coming and will let you in."

The elevator, thickly painted in an even darker shade of brown than that of the sheriff's department uniforms, wheezed up the three flights to the jail. The keeper was indeed waiting, peering through the tiny, grimy, wire-reinforced window in the heavy steel door. On seeing the Canon he opened the door, relocking it immediately after Bothwell's entry. As wiry as the dispatcher was corpulent, the jailer led the priest into the cell area, locking that door behind them, and heading down the corridor between the barred-off areas.

"I put him down here at the end so maybe the two of you could hear yourselves think," the jailer chirped. "It's Saturday night, and we got a couple of fraternity boys from the college that Dean Poole hasn't come down to collect yet, and some of the local talent has gotten pretty drunk, too. I don't know which is worse, hearing songs about Lambda Chi or being serenaded with revival hymns. When you want out, you'll have to yell loud enough to be heard over them," he said as he closed the cell door behind the professor.

The Canon saw the cell was simple. The floor was aged, unpainted cement, the back and only solid wall was institutional green to about shoulder height, and above that a curdled cream color spread upwards and onto the ceiling. The only place to sit other than the lidless porcelain toilet was the bunk lowered from the barred wall, its steel frame covered by a thin mattress. The upper bunk was folded up and had no mattress, suggesting that overcrowding would not be a problem. Everything was old but mercifully clean.

Seth sat on the bunk, elbows on his knees and face in his hands. The Canon sat beside him and, putting a comforting hand on his shoulder, said, "I am afraid that things are very unpleasant for you."

"Oh, Canon, it's all so different from what I imagined." Sitting up, Seth leaned back against the wall, hands in his pockets. "I've never told you about my call to the priesthood, have I? It came after I'd escaped from the prison camp in Vietnam. The survival training we had received in Special Forces made it relatively easy for us to live off the country. It was almost like being on patrol, except that you were alone, unarmed and had to try even harder to stay out of sight. It took about three weeks for me to work my way back to our territory—to the extent that we really controlled any of the country. I would have managed fine except for one thing: the gooks had this neat trick of decorating trails with punji traps, and I didn't see one until it was too late. I got a sharpened bamboo stake through the tire tread sole of the sandals they gave me in prison and it apparently had been dipped in excrement. At any rate, my heel got horribly infected. I had to walk with a crutch I made out of bamboo. But I was in and out of so much jungle water that it didn't have a chance. My foot and leg swelled up and turned purple, and I went out of my head with fever. Finally, I got off the trail in a place where I was pretty well hidden and laid down to die.

"When I passed out, Jesus appeared to me in a vision. I know that sounds pretty dramatic, but most of us in prison prayed a lot, and it seemed perfectly natural at the time. He told me that he wasn't going to let me die, because he still had some work for me to do. When I woke up, the swelling had gone way down. What woke me up was the sound of American voices. I was closer to the lines than I thought, and some Green Berets were on patrol. They took me back with them.

"That vision made me think that I was something special. I couldn't wait to get home and started in seminary. And I can't tell you what Sheila's letters meant to me when I was in prison. Not many of them got through, but the two of them that did were the only thing that sustained me in the torture and filth, except for God and my buddies there in prison.

"As you know, things haven't gone so well for us since we got here. And she had to get mixed up with that creep Sebastian. And I haven't shined so brightly as a student, either. As they say, pride goeth before a fall. And now I'm in jail again because they think I killed a bastard who really deserved killing, and I don't have any way of proving I didn't."

By this time Seth was pausing to control sobs, and his shoulders were hunched in an effort to hold in the despair that convulsed him. Roderick Bothwell put an arm around his shoulder and said, "Let it come, son. Don't hold it back. It's nothing to be ashamed of." For several minutes Seth wept, unable to restrain his tears any longer. The Canon thought that the tragic stature of his weeping was, in some curious way, more manly than all his effort to control his emotion. There was something Job-like and epic in the completeness of his sorrow. And then, as quickly as they came, his tears were over. He took the handkerchief extended to him by the priest, wiped his eyes, and sat up straight. He looked ready for whatever came.

The Canon put his handkerchief back into his hip pocket, took another from the breast pocket of his coat, and began to polish his glasses. "I feel confident that we will be able to establish your innocence. What worries me more than anything else right now are the strained relations between your wife and you. You will need her support in the ordeal ahead. Would you care to tell me anything about what went wrong between you? Maybe I can help."

"Canon, I would if I could, but I'm not at all certain that I know myself. I think a lot of it though is a result of my lack of experience with girls."

"Oh?"

"Yeah. Sounds funny, doesn't it? I know that people used to think that I really must be some kind of Romeo, first because I was an athlete, and then because I was a soldier. But I never did get over being very shy. And I guess having to spend so much time at sports practice when I was in school and trying to make good grades the rest of the time, I never did have much exposure to girls."

"That sometimes happens."

"Yeah, well, there was more to it than that. I think I must have had the idea there were two kinds of girls—nice ones who would grow up to be like my mother and her friends, and those who weren't. And I felt that what my body wanted to do would have horrified any girl that I liked and would get serious about. It horrified me, and I tried not to think about it. I'll never forget the first time I went to a whorehouse. Purdue was playing Indiana, and I went with one of my teammates after the game. I was so badly embarrassed that I was barely able to perform, and when I finished I went outside and threw up. But I had learned the ropes and went back whenever the pressure got too bad. As available as it was in 'Nam, I always thought it was wrong and stayed away as much as I could. Anyway, when I got married, that was all the experience I had, and the only way I knew to use Sheila was like a whore. We had a couple of days of honeymoon and were so much in love that I guess she was able to overcome her revulsion. Anyway, it didn't really start to cause trouble until I got back."

"I see. I take it that you did not have any sisters."

"No, nor brothers either, for that matter. Nor even a father who was an effective force in my life. He left my mother when I was just a baby. He was a doctor and ran away with his nurse to California. He established a good practice out there and always supported us well, but I don't remember seeing him until I went out there in preparation for being sent overseas. Then he was just a stranger. My mother hadn't thought much of him. He drank, she said, and ran around. Being alone in the world together, my mother and I were pretty close, and I knew that the last thing in the world that she wanted was for me to grow up and be like him."

"I'm a little surprised that being as close to your mother as you were, you became such an athlete and outdoorsman. Were those interests of hers?"

"No, the French class, dancing lessons, and being a choir boy and acolyte were the things I did that she was proud of. It was the other boys who forced me into sports. When I was in the third grade some of them started calling me 'sissy' and 'momma's little baby.' When they ganged up on me, I had to defend myself the best I knew how. I discovered that I was pretty coordinated, and I was tall and strong for my age, so I surprised them and myself by how well I could fight, and I also discovered that I liked it. Still, it took some doing to get her to approve. I began by getting involved in the Scouts, which was respectable enough for her. Football horrified her, so I played basketball, except for my freshman year at Purdue. And I had to keep my grades up, or she would never have let me go out for sports."

Bothwell took a notebook out of his pocket. "That reminds me," he said. "Shouldn't I try to inform your wife and your mother about this contretemps?"

"No. Honestly, I don't know where to reach Sheila, but I guess she'll be coming home tomorrow anyway. And my mother died when I was overseas. I don't have any other close relatives."

"Then is there anything else I could do to help you tonight?"

"I guess not, Canon, other than praying for me. I need it bad."

"I see that you do."

"But you don't know all of it. Canon, the reason I busted out of that prison was that I couldn't stand it anymore. They had tortured me so much and made me do so many things I didn't think that I would ever do that I was ready to take my own life if I had to stay there much longer. Now I know that this jail isn't like that, and they don't treat you the same way, but I'm afraid that the associations are so strong that I just won't be able to take it."

"That's very understandable. I will not only pray for you now, but will also make you the chief intention of my own prayers tonight and for the Eucharist in the morning."

"Canon, I can't tell you how much I appreciate this support you're giving me. But there's one more thing you better know. Canon, I think that what I told the sheriff is true, but I can't be certain. I blacked out last night, I was that drunk. My memory covers all I said pretty well, but it's spotty at first and then blanks out altogether. I don't remember going to bed, and so, of course, don't know what I did just before."

# 8

At 8:30 the next morning, the Canon left the elevator on the jail floor of the courthouse, bundled in his dark gray herringbone tweed topcoat, clerical collar almost obscured by his scarf in the clergy tartan, gray homburg with black band slightly slanted forward to accommodate the enormous dome of his skull, and creased trouser legs neatly folded into the tops of his buckle-fastening overshoes. A Prayer Book was clasped in his grey suede glove. Bothwell moved purposely down the aisle after the jailer, leaving his fellow passenger on the elevator to follow behind them. When they came to Seth's cell, they found him at the window staring out, looking almost naked by the simple absence of a belt around his waist and laces in his combat boots. As he turned to see who was entering his cell, Bothwell found it amazing and touching that someone who had been through so much could still look child-like and vulnerable.

"Good morning, Seth. I've brought the Sacrament to you, and I also have someone here who is going to help you."

Removing his hat and gloves and placing them on the cot, he also opened his coats and removed a black leather pouch from his inside jacket pocket, letting it hang on its black cord around his neck as he opened the book. "We will start with the General Confession. 'In the name of the Father and the Son and the Holy Ghost . . .'" And so it went, the boy holding out his large, strong hands crossed to receive the frail wafer of Christ at the proper time and raising it to his mouth, but doing so as though dazed or in a dream. After the thanksgiving and blessing, Bothwell restored the silver pyx to the pouch and the pouch to his pocket. Only then did he introduce the man who had followed him into the cell and stood attentively while the Sacrament was being administered.

"Mr. Hoover, this is the young man I was telling you about, Mr. Seth Clarke. Seth, I would like for you to meet Mr. Virgil Hoover. Mr. Hoover is a vestryman at St. John's and an attorney here in town. I believe that he is not only the best trial lawyer in Montgomery County, but one of the best admitted to plead before the Indiana Supreme Court. I called him after I got home last night, and he agreed to attend the early service this morning and come here with me afterwards. He is willing to represent you if you do not have your own attorney."

Seth shook the outstretched hand of the man who was only an inch or so short of his own 6'4' and who must have weighed twenty pounds more without any appearance of softness. Except for a few strands pulled neatly across the open space of the top of his head, his black hair was trimmed short. The tortoise rims of his glasses looked assertive without the aggressiveness of the heavy ones favored by Senator Goldwater and pre-Beatles pop musicians. His features were heavy but not coarse, and there was a slight red tint to his face that looked almost like a reflection of the regimental striped tie under the button-down collar of the blue oxford shirt.

Seth said, "I'm pleased to meet you, sir. The only lawyer I've ever had to deal with settled my mother's estate when I was overseas. I don't know him and don't feel that I have much call on him. I'm going to need all the help I can get. I'd appreciate it very much if you would defend me, but I don't know how much help I can be."

"Let me worry about that," the lawyer replied. "Let's get the formalities out of the way first. You may want the Canon to leave while we do this. Your answer will not affect my decision to represent you, but I need to know this: did you kill the Seymour fellow?"

"The Canon can hear anything I have to say, because I have a feeling he is the best friend I have right now. But it really makes no difference in this instance. I didn't kill Sebastian. I didn't even see him night before last."

"Okay, I thought not. It's a formality I had to go through. You are supposed innocent until proven guilty. But in a case like this with lots of circumstantial evidence against you, it's going to be as if the burden of proof is on us. I'll come by tomorrow and go over the whole deal with you in detail, so that I'll know what to start working on. At the moment, though, about all we need is to go over interrogation. You needn't worry about the Sheriff. He's as straight as they come. He will not try to trap you into anything, but he will notice inconsistencies in what you say, and he'll try to find out what's behind them. You are entitled to have me with you if you want me. My guess is that you don't need me. You won't tell them anything but the truth, and I have a feeling that it's going to take every bit of information we can muster to get you out of this thing. We need to expose the truth, not to suppress it."

"I'll tell them everything I know, but it won't be much."

"Good boy. Remember that the Sheriff probably doesn't want you to be guilty, but I imagine that appearances are so strong against you that they overwhelm him. And even thinking you're guilty, he still probably wants to be on your side. We haven't had too many heroes in this country lately, and we want to hold on to all we have. I'll see you tomorrow."

The phone call in midafternoon was from Jane Spruling, the Clarke's next-door neighbor. "Dr. Bothwell," she said, "I thought you ought to know that Sheila Clarke just drove up. I saw her through the front window, but I didn't go out. It seems better for her to learn from somebody else."

The Canon bundled up immediately and went across to the Hutches. Just as he turned up the Clarke's walk, Sheila was coming out the door.

"If you're looking for Seth, Canon Bothwell, he's not here. I don't know where he is. In fact, I just got in and was going next door to see if the Sprulings had any idea of where he might be."

"That is what I have come about, Mrs. Clarke. Perhaps we should go inside. I'm afraid I don't have good news for you."

Going back inside, Sheila asked, "Don't tell me that he has gone and gotten himself in bad with the seminary. I'm not surprised. The apartment looks like he must have been on a binge. All the dishes are where I left them on the drain board, so he must not have eaten here. But there's a half-emptied bottle of bourbon by the bed, and the bed's rumpled, and it looks like someone threw up in the john and did a poor job of cleaning it up. But he must have slept it off and gone out somewhere after that. I don't know where. He didn't leave a note."

"Sit down, Mrs. Clarke. You are right. Seth did get drunk when he learned your plans for the weekend, but the trouble he is in is far worse than that, and it does not just concern the seminary. The news does not seem to have been released to the press yet. When it is, you will undoubtedly be besieged by journalists and television people—far more than you have ever had to cope with before. Mrs. Clarke, Mr. Seymour was found dead yesterday morning, and the police believe that your husband is responsible, and they are holding him in the county jail in Crawfordsville."

The Canon watched as the most perfectly constructed face he had ever seen came apart before him. It was like watching the demolition of an architectural monument. The already fair complexion became ghostly, the cornflower eyes behind the long lashes and under the elegant brows were first opened widely and then clouded over. Mascara began to run. The waxy perfection of the lips was twisted like a racecar in a collision.

"What have I done?" she gasped as she hunched her back and bent her head into her hands.

The Canon reached out a hand to comfort. "Mrs. Clarke, I do not think any blame for the death of Mr. Seymour rests on your shoulders."

The svelte spine immediately snapped straight, sparks struck from the steel blue eyes, the face restored into an entity. "Don't be silly! Of course they fought over me!"

The soothing hand recoiled. "Mrs. Clarke, I meant only to say that the identity of Mr. Seymour's killer is unknown, and that I am convinced that your husband is not the guilty party."

As quickly as Sheila had sprouted into life she now wilted, tears and sobs coming down like a mountain river at spring thaw. "Oh, Father, I'm horrible. All my life I've been revolted by the things that boys do, but I've always known that I could make them do them, and I have enjoyed watching them jump when I snapped my fingers."

Again she pulled herself together, but now into a less erect, a less distinct configuration. Even her features seemed to be less etched, more blurred as her face took on an air of desolation. "But that doesn't mean that Seth didn't do it. Canon, you don't know how far I pushed him, how near the edge he was. I must have been punishing him for letting his vocation mean more to him than I did, but I was hateful, I was bitchy. I could see the anger building. And, Canon, he is a killer. Haven't you read how he got that Medal of Honor? He was a maniac, a death machine. That one time he killed twenty-three men all by himself! I know he did it."

"Mrs. Clarke, I know that your husband is worried sick about you. May I take you to see him?"

"See him? I couldn't. He will kill me. He hates me." Drawing up her knees onto the couch, she hugged them, looking furtively from one corner of the room to another. Again she was overwhelmed by tears and fell into the cushions at the corner of the couch. "I'm going to call my daddy. He'll come and get me and take me home. Daddy will take care of me."

Going next door, the Canon said, "Mrs. Spruling, could you stay with Mrs. Clarke for a little while? She has had a bad shock. I am going to call Dr. Evans to come and give her a sedative. Then I will get Frank and Katrina to drive her to her home in Effingham. I'm sure that the sheriff will want to talk to her, but that can wait until she is past the immediate trauma of this news. Please try to get the phone number of her family home for me. That would not be in our records."

It had been four hours since Horace brought Seth down the jail elevator to the sheriff's office, and Wade Bryant had read to the seminarian the small Miranda warning encased in plastic that he took from his billfold. Having answered that he did understand that he could remain silent, that what he said could be used against him in a court, that his lawyer could be present, and that the court would appoint him a lawyer if he could not afford one, Seth said that he was willing to talk to the peace officers then.

His willingness, however, had been no guarantee of a mutually satisfactory outcome. Every detail had been gone over a hundred times. Yes, he had threatened to kill Sebastian. Yes, he had gone looking for him. No, he had not found him. Yes, he had gone to the chapel. If they said that Sebastian's body had been found there, they knew better than he. Certainly he knew how to strike a karate blow on the back of the neck so that it could break someone's neck. But, no, Sebastian had not entered the chapel while he was there. When he left the chapel he went straight to the apartment he shared with his wife and remained there until the sheriff and his deputy had arrived the night before.

Seth by now had made a complete inventory of the furnishings of the sheriff's office from memory. The large grey steel desk was functional but of good quality. The stack of wire trays did not appear reserved for "in" and "out" separation, but as receptacles for wanted posters, ticket books, other government forms, law enforcement periodicals, and documents for which no one could decide the appropriate filing category. There was even a crayon greeting card for Grandpa on Father's Day. The wall had a few framed certificates, the Rotary "Four-Way Test," an autographed picture of the governor, and a rough-and-ready montage of glossy photographs taken at the scenes of crimes and wrecks. A steel bookcase held law books, criminal investigation textbooks, government publications, catalogs, and phone books spread so sparsely over the shelves that all of the spines were damaged from being stored in leaning positions over long periods of time. Turn-of-the-century architectural details—the mosaic pattern of the tile floor, the golden oak door with its frosted glass window and decorated brass knob, the large windows that let in the afternoon sun—seemed inconsistent with the gray steel and fake wood-grained plastic of the furnishings, as though an aristocratic female ancestor had shown up in a polyester pants suit. Efforts at cleaning had obviously hit the high spots and ignored the corners at the county's expense.

The legal pad on the sheriff's desk retained a virginal freshness, and he had long since put down the county-issue ballpoint pen that he held in readiness to note down significant disclosures. His large right hand lay on the desk, two fingers slowly drumming. Sunlight caught the rose-gold gleam of the hairs on the back of the hand, showed up numerous freckles, and cast small shadows behind the veins.

After a long pause he said, "Son, we're getting nowhere. It keeps coming out the same. You say you didn't do it and don't know anything about it. You don't seem aware of how damning the case against you is. You yourself admit that you uttered a threat against his life shortly before he was killed. You admit that you know how to inflict a wound like his with the edge of your hand. You were at the right place at what is at least very close to the right time. A matchstick that you chewed was found under his body.

"We are dealing here with a sealed room. That new snow means that we know how many people went in and out of the chapel from midnight on. One set of tracks led from the dormitory to the chapel. That had to be Seymour. Another led out of the chapel and down the campus. It was in just about the same shape as the tracks up to your front door when we arrived last night. Only Seymour and you could have been in that chapel when he died.

"And there is nothing in that whole chapel that could have been used as a weapon. Whatever struck that blow must have been taken out by the person who used it. Your hand could have inflicted that damage, and you know how to use it.

"Son, I don't see any possible theory that fits all these facts other than that you killed that boy. Now, I don't know as I blame you. In the circumstances I might have done the same thing. And everything else I know about you I admire. But the fact remains that my duty is to charge you with murder and let the court decide what, if anything, should be done about it. I imagine that a jury would even be more sympathetic if you admitted that you had done it like the man you are. What do you say?"

Seth turned from his inspection of a crack in the plaster to face the sheriff, for the first time really establishing contact between his gray eyes and the sheriff's hazel ones. "I see very clearly how bad it looks for me, and I know you mean well, but I can't say that I did anything I didn't do. You and the court have your duty to do, and you have to do it, but I did not kill Sebastian Seymour, however much he deserved killing."

The sheriff stood up and began buckling on the holster belt that he had removed for comfort. Pulling on his jacket and reaching for his hat, he said, "Okay, the only thing I know to do now is to take you to Lafayette tomorrow and let the State Police run a polygraph on you. When you have it proved that you're lying, maybe you will cooperate. Take him back to his cell, Horace."

Highway 231 from Crawfordsville to Lafayette is narrow, curved, and hilly. Its half-hour exposure to Indiana farmland bore no interest to Seth as the sheriff's car sped along, even though the snow lent a Currier and Ives atmosphere to all they passed. It would have seemed, had he noticed, that the drive through Lafayette past billboards, frame houses, and Purdue took almost as long as getting to the city had. Finally, they were on Interstate 65 and then at the State Police headquarters. The building was one of those modern office structures that Seth thought of as "plastic," planned for obsolescence and replacement. He and Horace were left in a waiting room while the sheriff went up to brief the trooper who would conduct the interview. When Bryant returned half an hour later, he brought with him an Asian-looking man of medium height. Surprisingly for the time of year, the man's suit was a light tan polyester, his shirt a pale yellow wash-and-wear material, and his tie a dark, rusty brown silk. The impression of neatness and cleanliness was total. Even though the Asian's normal expression seemed to be a smile that lit up his whole face, Seth began to tremble when he saw him.

The sheriff said, "Seth, this is Sergeant Fong. He will take you upstairs and interview you with the polygraph. He's been specially trained to do that, and he conducts all our interviews in this part of the state." Getting off the elevator, they passed through the detective division in which there were numerous desks in the center of a large room and others in cubicles partitioned off on the sides. At a third of the desks troopers in plain clothes sat reading, writing out reports, or interviewing someone. The interrogation room used for polygraph had solid walls instead of partitions; there were windows that looked out onto the hall on either side of the door, and another large window of frosted glass was set into the wall away from the corner. In the center of the ten-by-ten room was a steel office table with a Formica top. An office chair was on each of the long sides of the table. At one end of the table was what looked like a small leather-grained suitcase with metal reinforced corners; it was not unlike the field communion sets used by chaplains in Vietnam.

Removing the handcuffs from Seth with a key he had been given by Horace, the sergeant told him to sit. Then he explained the procedure. "The test is based on a recognition that lying usually produces involuntary stress in an individual. The polygraph monitors signs of that stress by plotting graphs of a subject's blood pressure, breath patterns, and what we call galvanic skin response. That means that the amount of electrical resistance in a person's skin changes under stress, although nobody knows why. Anyway, that change of resistance is one of the things this machine records.

"I will ask you three kinds of questions, for all of which the answer will be yes or no. The first kind will be about things you know, but in which you have no emotional investment, like I'll say, 'Is the color of your hair black?' Then I will ask you some questions that are control questions, questions about the sort of thing that most of us do and are embarrassed about, so that we tend to lie. For instance, I might ask, 'Have you ever masturbated?' I do that to get a pattern of what the graphs look like when you lie. And then I will ask some questions about the things we really want to know. It's almost impossible to beat the machine. When you lie, it will show up.

"Okay, now look, we're trying to learn something from this. We want to know whether you're lying or not. It won't help us to catch you off balance or do something that might obscure the results. We do this in a 'no surprises' way. I'll even tell you in advance the whole list of questions I'm going to ask before we hook you up on the machine. So just relax, we're not going to try to put anything over on you. Now the first set of questions I'm going to ask you goes like this . . ."

The list as read conformed rigidly to the criteria the sergeant had spelled out and, had he been able to concentrate of doing so, Seth could have categorized each of them as he mumbled his affirmative and negative responses. As Fong took the cover off the case, plugged the unit into the wall receptacle with an extension cord, and placed graph paper under the needles, the movement of his jacket front revealed the bright plaid lining under the sedate exterior and also furnished occasional glimpses of the snub-nosed Smith and Wesson Detective Special in a small holster on his belt to the left. As he tied the pneumograph tube around Seth's chest, Fong was aware of trembling, and when he affixed the blood pressure cuff to his arm, he could see beads of perspiration.

An hour and a half later, looking tired and even a little rumpled, he locked the interrogation room door on Seth and went in the next room down the hall where the sheriff and Horace were seated at the two-way window looking at their prisoner.

"Well," said the sergeant, "you've seen what it's been like. He's even reacted to the irrelevant questions. I don't think I've ever seen anybody so upset by the test. It's hard to believe that this man is a hero. I'm afraid that from our point of view, this test is inconclusive. It wouldn't be admitted as evidence. All I can say is that you have one scared cookie on your hands."

# 9

For an hour after lights out Seth had lain on his cot listening. There were only five other prisoners—two drunks, a kid caught prying open gum machines with a jimmy, a wife-beater, and a pimp—and they were all down the hall. Several cells away from Seth there was even a wall between them and him. Still, he wanted to be sure that they and the jailer were asleep. When all had been quiet for some time, he got up off his cot very gingerly so that the chain supporting it would not rattle, and the pivot that permitted it to swivel up did not squeak. Then, pulling up the left leg of his khakis and his thermal-knit long johns, he untaped the flat surgical steel knife that had been one of the first purchases he had made after his escape from the Vietnamese prison six months before, and which he had worn taped to the inside of his shin ever since as something between a talisman and insurance. Luckily, the frisk they gave him when he was brought in had been perfunctory.

At that time his first act, once left alone, had been to inspect the window in his cell. Being in a cell again gave him a strong sense of déjà vu. He had almost tapped out a message on the wall to find out if other Americans were kept there, and who the senior ranking officer was, until he had reminded himself he was in an American jail. The prisoners could openly communicate with one another and would not be abused or tortured. There were probably no rats, and he saw no stocks at the end of the cot.

The windowsill was about five feet off the floor so that he could rest his elbows on it when his upper arms were slightly below the horizontal. A wooden frame was fitted into the opening in the plaster-covered brick, and upper and lower sashes could be moved up or down with a good bit of effort and some noise. Behind this were the bars. Steel rods an inch in diameter had been set six inches apart in a frame of quarter-inch flat steel that was three inches wide. All that held the bars was mortar, and the mortar seemed to have deteriorated in the eighty years since the courthouse had been built.

Possibly the window frames obscured the view of this diminishment of security, or perhaps the county, lulled by the infrequence of escape attempts, had just assumed that no man in his right mind would try to climb out of a third-story window. Those not in their right minds went into the padded cell. Seth had found that the mortar gave way in time to his knife.

In the safe hours of his first two nights in captivity, he had been able to chip away the mortar around the steel frame along the bottom and up the sides to about four inches above the lower window, as far as he could reach standing on the floor. He had been slowed down in his efforts by the need not to rub his knuckles so raw that they would attract attention and raise questions. His experience of chipping holes in Vietnamese prison walls had taught him patience. Here he did not even have the problem of disposing of his dust or covering up where he had been working. He had also begun work in strategic spots around the upper side of the frame, since he knew that working through the upper half of the window required him to brace his knees against the wall and hold his weight off the floor and against the window with one arm reached over the sashes and wrapped around the bars while the other hand was driving the knife into the mortar, something that he could do for only a few seconds at a time, and then at widely spaced intervals. Here too he ran a serious risk of noise.

Having accomplished so much previously, he worked only an hour before testing the bars. Raising both sashes so that he could grasp the bars firmly with both hands while standing on the floor, he lunged, putting as much arm and back muscle and as much body weight as possible into his effort to dislodge the grill. There was a lot of promising give, but he put in another hour with the knife before he tried again. Three lunges and the frame came loose, and he was grabbing fast to keep the heavy steel from clanging down against the side of the building. With some effort he wrestled it inside. The first part of the job was done.

Next he pulled the blankets from the bed. His first night he had complained to the jailer that he was cold in order to get a second army blanket. Sitting on the cot, he folded one of the blankets lengthwise and held the two edges on the top taunt in his left hand while he sawed through the center crease with the knife. When he had finally worked his way down the length of the covering, he laid one side on his lap and doubled the other and began his cutting operation once again. A full moon gave him as much light as he needed, but to someone with his experience of working in the dark, the task of keeping the cut straight by feel alone would have been simple.

Eventually the job was done: he had sixteen strips of wool blanketing about six inches wide and six feet long. A six-inch width would bear his body weight with a good safety margin, he thought. Square knots seemed better than fisherman knots, but his life would depend on his not tying a granny by mistake. The last strip was cut in two to make wrap leggings that would hold his combat boots on.

He had no choice but to go out the window headfirst. He was certain that the architect had kept the two cots more than his body's length from the window precisely to avoid being helpful to anyone with intentions similar to his own. He had run one end of the blanket rope around one of the bars on the hall side of the cell and pulled it out even with the other end, making a double cord; at first he had thought he would use the end of the upper bunk but the chances of the line's fouling seemed greater there. Then he wrapped the double line around his body in the "hot seat" rappel position, wishing as heartily for carabineers as he did for a nylon rope. He had left enough slack on the rappel sling to enable him to get out the window. Wriggling through did require enormous effort, even to someone in as good a shape as Seth, since the part of the line that was over his shoulder was the free-hanging part that he had already thrown out the window. When he had arms and waist through and could hang over the window ledge with his body doubled, he had to reach his left hand back through his legs to grasp the secured end of the line. Then he had to push against the wall with his right hand so that his legs came through the window. There was a ticklish moment when his legs came tumbling out, and he did a somersault and fell free until all the slack on the left end of the line had been taken up. Maybe he would have done better to use a hasty rappel for the jail floor of the courthouse, but he had been uncertain of the height. When his feet caught against the side of the building, he relaxed and began to pay out the line, grateful that the training at Fort Bragg had been so vigorous, and that rappelling was a necessary part of Special Forces preparation. The knots in the line slowed progress, but that was probably just as well since he had no gloves to protect himself from rope burn.

He had twenty feet of roof to walk across at the foot of the jail story. Crouching low, he went along the edge of the roof until he came to an entrance on the side of the building out of the range of streetlights. The entrance was only one story tall, but the design of the portico over it called for matching stonework on the roofline of the second story where Seth was. A projecting piece of this looked secure enough for him to loop his doubled line over. The town was very quiet. No cars were on the street. All the room lights at the Crawford Hotel were out. With a quick prayer he started down again. Even though this leg of the journey was more than twice as long as the first, it was a piece of cake. He came down into a space between ornamental shrubs and the wall so that he was hidden as he pulled his line down.

By then he had begun to feel the cold. As planned, he wrapped his body in a cocoon of blanket strips, saving enough for a turban, but leaving his limbs unimpeded, since he knew that they were almost insignificant in the economics of body heat. He did, however, wrap a section of a band around each hand. Then he began to walk in the direction of Wabash College, keeping in the shadows and preferring alleys to streets. He saw only one car moving during the seven-block walk, but luckily it turned the other way when it came to his intersection. He would have been invisible anyway, so quickly did he find cover in shrubbery. Across the street from the campus he found what he had been looking for, one of several two-story frat houses with a neon sign over the door delineating three Greek letters and illuminating an ornate court of arms below. As he expected, several bicycles were on the porch. The best ten-speed was locked, but the second-best was not. Quietly lifting it to the sidewalk, he mounted and went down a side street, following others like it and alleys, breaking cover only when he had to cross the bridge over Sugar Creek. Luck stayed with him, and he was out of town on the Yountsville road by three o'clock.

Bothwell, having been awakened at 6:15 by a phone call from Horace informing him of Seth's escape, was at the Clarke apartment twenty minutes later when the deputy and his boss arrived. Again the deputy went around to the back door while the sheriff knocked on the front door, his .38 caliber Police Special drawn and ready. The bluing was worn in places, but it was well oiled and well cared for. Nothing fancy, a craftsman's tool, simple and efficient. The bare utilitarianism of the weapon made it more horrifying to the Canon and the event more surreal—a gun drawn on a postulant for holy orders and drawn more in sadness than anger.

"If you're in there, son," the sheriff said, "come on out and give yourself up. We don't want to hurt you."

There was no response from the apartment in which they were interested, although doors opened and curtains were drawn back in others. A mother pulled back into the house a preschooler who had just walked out the door, bundled in snow pants, parka, and muffler.

The sheriff called again, and still there was no response. The third time he knocked louder and called into the door, "Son, if you don't come out, I'm gon' have to come in." When there was still no reply, he turned to the Canon.

"He's probably not in there and may not even have come here, but I'm going to have to find out. I had already asked the judge yesterday for a search warrant for the house, and so I can go in. I don't suppose you have a key for the apartment?"

"No, but I doubt if it's locked. Almost no one locks anything up around here. Why don't you just try the door?"

Doing so, the sheriff found that it opened easily and went inside, motioning to the Canon to remain where he was. His footsteps could be heard as he went slowly and systematically through the house. Bothwell heard the doors of closets and the bathroom open and close, as the sound of the sheriff's footsteps diminished with the distance. Then the feet could be heard moving back at a normal pace.

"He's not here now, but he's been here. Lot of blanket strips knotted together in the middle of the living room floor. I figured that must have been the way he climbed down the walls." Calling to the deputy who had just come around the end of the building, the sheriff said, "Horace, call the State Police and tell 'em to set up roadblocks and start a manhunt. I guess we can get copies made of that picture on his wife's dresser. Except for the uniform, he hasn't changed much in appearance. Reverend, do you know if his car is here?"

The Canon looked down the sidewalk to the parking area by the street. "Yes, I believe that white Volkswagen is his, the one that looks like a small station wagon. His wife was driven to her family home in my car the day before yesterday."

"Okay, if we're looking for a car, we're looking for one that he stole in town. We'll have to wait and see if any get reported missing." It was several days before the strange bike in the rear rack near the Hutches was noticed, reported, and identified.

When the Canon had completed his nine o'clock lecture, he was met at the classroom door by the Dean's secretary, who informed him that the Dean wanted to see him immediately. Going downstairs he noted a number of strangers were standing around in the hall. Others filled the Dean's outer office. Most of them were no older than seminarians and wore similar if more expensive clothing. Longish hair, beards on the men, all smoking, some with notebooks, but most with cameras ranging from SLR 35's to heavy movie types with decals on the side stating channel numbers, call letters, and networks.

The Dean responded to the knock on the door by almost pulling him into his office. "Come in, Bothwell. What took you so long? This is terrible. The place is swarming with reporters. I hope we can get them away from here before they start taking pictures of some of the grubbier-looking students. Look, is there any way that we can soft-pedal the fact that Clarke and Seymour were students here? Say that they were part-time or something?"

"I am afraid not, Mr. Dean, since you held a press conference the day we received Mr. Clarke's application and told many of these same press people that the greatest hero of the Vietnam war had chosen Chase out of all the available seminaries as the best place to study for the ministry. I think there was also a feature story in the *Star* about how the ex-assistant of the Reverend Bob Smith was going to study for the Episcopal priesthood. If memory serves, the article said that he had been accepted here."

"My God, Bothwell, what am I going to do? Those reporters are not just from Crawfordsville and Lafayette. All of the Indianapolis papers and TV stations are represented out there, and I even had a call from a Chicago station. There's no way we can keep word of this from the people we depend on for support."

"Mr. Dean, I think we should remind everyone that in this country a person is innocent until proven guilty. Besides, I believe that the majority of the people will be very sympathetic to Mr. Clarke. He is a famous hero for whom many have a great deal of admiration and, even if he were guilty, he would have acted in accordance with what is widely considered to be an unwritten law. I think that we should take a position that he is a student in good standing here until he has been found guilty by a court of law. I am sure that our supporters would like to see us firm on a matter of both Christian and American principle."

"I suppose you're right. I'd better go through with it. Here, let me put my gown on. Is my hair combed?"

In mid-afternoon Sheila returned in response to a request from the sheriff that she look through Seth's things in hopes that the discovery of what was missing could lead to some conclusion about his escape plans. She was driven from Effingham by her father, a dentist who had never been able to refuse his beautiful daughter anything, especially after her mother died of lung cancer when Sheila was in eighth grade. The girl had somehow managed to avoid going through any of the awkward, all knees and elbows or all ears and teeth periods that most children go through. Her looks had become the focus for family activity, and she had been enrolled in classes in singing or dancing in kindergarten. Even though she showed no particular aptitude for either, the recitals that accompanied them furnished occasions in which she could appear on stage in costumes created by the best local seamstress. By the time her mother died, she had already spent several years being tutored in baton twirling, and it was natural that her high school years should be spent in front of the band in a series of sequined outfits, tossing batons, flags, torches, and even knives into the air and usually catching them. At Champaign-Urbana, being a drum majorette did not have enough status, so her sorority had groomed her from the beginning to become homecoming queen. Through it all, Dr. Davidson had been there to beam proudly at his daughter, to be introduced when it seemed to suit her and to fade into the background when it did not, and always to sign the checks in whatever amount was prescribed.

Now as always he stood on the sidelines, wondering if she should be doing so much, but not wishing to run the risk of rebuke by saying so. Sheila, however, looked very unlike her normal self. Wearing no makeup and dressed in old jeans and a sweater, she went through the apartment as though in a daze, doing the task assigned to her as conscientiously as possible. When she had completed her inventory she told the sheriff that Seth had taken things mainly for camping. His backpack was gone, for instance. She said that he had a "thing" about survival and had kept it packed with articles for staying alive in the woods, such as halazone tablets for water purification, fishing line and hooks, a fancy slingshot, some nylon cord, that sort of thing. His hiking boots, always kept snow-proofed and over which he was quite fussy, were also gone, and his dirty combat boots were back in the apartment. His down sleeping bag, which was supposed to keep him warm at twenty below zero, had also been taken, as well as his expensive archery equipment and his hand axe in the leather case that buckled onto his belt. Little clothing other than his down parka and gloves seemed to be gone. He appeared to have changed clothes without showering, an unusual practice for him. Very little food had been taken and none of his firearms— not a handgun, shotgun, or rifle was missing from the rack.

After the search was completed, and the sheriff had thanked her and left, Dr. Davidson suggested to Sheila that they should be heading back to Effingham before it got too late; but she surprised him by saying that she would stay. She did have a job and would need to get to work the next day. He made some effort to dissuade her, but it became obvious that her decision was firm. She would not even let him stay and take her out to a nice dinner in Crawfordsville. With reluctance he got into the big Olds 98 alone and drove toward the highway.

Roderick Bothwell had telephoned Tom Wright at three o'clock to say that he had a question of importance to discuss with him and to ask if he were free for a drink after Evensong. He had been, and so they had met afterwards and walked down campus to faculty row together. Bothwell kept the conversation firmly on incidental subjects until they were seated in his parlor, and Tom held a Waterford tumbler full of ice and Virginia Gentlemen, and the Canon was sipping some Pedro Domeq and nibbling on a toasted almond from the silver bowl on the table between them. When they were thus settled, Bothwell was ready to open his mind.

"Tom," he said, "I am worried about the way that the sheriff's office is going about the investigation."

"What concerns you? From what I've heard, they've been extremely considerate of young Clarke. He was not being abused. The manhunt seems like a necessity under the circumstances of his escape, and I don't have the impression gun-crazed killers are on his trail."

"No, the sheriff is a very honorable man and quite conscientious in the performance of his duty. I think that he had real admiration for Seth's war record, and that he would not blame him too much for disposing of Mr. Seymour. What worries me is the sheriff's inability to consider any explanation of Seymour's death other than that Seth killed him."

"Well, Rod, you'll have to admit that the evidence against him is pretty overwhelming."

"No, Tom, that's exactly what I will not admit. All the evidence is consistent with Seth's having done it, but none of it directly connects him with the crime."

"What about the 'sealed room' aspect of the case?"

"Even that does not show that Seth was in the chapel at the same time as Mr. Seymour. It only shows that each of them was there at some time after the snow began to fall. There is no physical evidence that directly links Seth to the crime."

"Well, who else could have done it?"

"That is precisely the question that the sheriff has not asked. Everything appears so consistent with Seth's having done it that there has been no effort to discover any other suspects. So far as I know, the sheriff has not even attempted to retrace Mr. Seymour's steps the evening before he died. He could have been with someone who would have been very happy to have him dead. From the little I know about his life before coming here, I can think of a number of people who might consider the world a better place without him. At least someone could find out what they were doing that evening."

"Rod, aren't you letting your sympathy for the boy run away with you?"

"No, Tom, I am not. Admittedly, I consider him to be incapable of murder for personal benefit, but here I am reacting from my most basic historiographical convictions. Criminal investigation is, after all, a form of historical reconstruction, and it is always bad methodologically to ask what might have been. An infinite number of things might have been. What we must ask is what we have physical evidence for supposing did happen. Without material evidence we have no certain link between the person and the event. We are left in the realm of conjecture. And no one should be convicted of a capital crime on the basis of conjecture."

"In the mystery stories that I read, Rod, the questions asked are motive, opportunity, and access to the weapon."

"What do we learn from them? Motive? That's the fallacy of Collingwood—to understand the event as an act of a human agent, before establishing that the human being in question was actually the agent of the event. Opportunity? At best that is but a possibility. The weapon? Again, we know only of access to a possible weapon. If we knew beyond the shadow of a doubt that Seth's hand had severed Mr. Seymour's spinal column, we would know that he was the wielder of the weapon, but we do not know that. To repeat, there is no physical evidence that connects Seth with Seymour's death."

"Rod, you're really involved in all of this, aren't you?"

"That's what I want to discuss with you, Tom. Since it appears the sheriff is not looking into any alternative explanations of the death of Mr. Seymour, I have decided that I must. He has better facilities for doing so than I, but he's not going to use any of them. My training in historiographical method may help. At least I know evidence when I see it—and the lack of evidence as well."

"All right, Rod. I had never thought of you as the Nero Wolfe type, but if this is something that you think you ought to do, you can count on me to back you up. I'll help out in any way that I can."

# 10

As Horace turned the sheriff's car off State 147 at the big sign proclaiming the entrance to Turkey Run State Park, he was aware of how beautiful the drive from Crawfordsville had been. The cold front ushered in by the snow had completely passed, and the weatherman had promised temperatures in the mid-30s for the day. Already the roads were completely clear, and the encroachment of the snow on the right of way was receding. The sky was blue and brilliant, and the tall evergreens along the road gleamed with a crisp clarity. It was the world of Kodachrome slides with all colors brighter and sharper than real life. The asphalt drive sparkled black where the melted snow was draining off in tiny rivulets that disappeared at the edge of the melting snow.

As they were waved on by the gate house attendant, Wade, who had said little during the twenty-mile drive from town, merely pointed with his hand toward the park office on the road to the right that wove its way toward the picnic grounds. Already the two units sent up by the State Patrol from Terre Haute were parked in front, their motors idling to keep their occupants warm.

When they pulled up beside the state cars, stopped the engine, and got out, Wade motioned to the troopers to follow him inside. To the secretary seated behind the counter inside the door, Wade said, "I am Sheriff Bryant. This is Lieutenant Harrison from the State Police. I believe the Property Manager is expecting us." She rose from her chair and walked through a door and into a hall.

"Yes, he is, Sheriff. Right this way." Standing at the first door to the right, she ushered the six men into the office, saying, "Mr. Hall, the sheriff is here to see about Seth." The man at the desk was wearing the uniform of the state park service. He stood and reached out a welcoming hand. He was of moderate height, a little plump, and had a roundish face in which dark eyes gleamed intelligently. Lines in his face suggested that he was normally a smiling, pleasant person, but now his features seemed weighed down by sadness and concern.

"Sit down, Sheriff. You, too, Lieutenant. I'll get some chairs for you other men."

"Don't bother, Mr. Hall," the sheriff said, "we don't want to take up too much of your time, and we do want to get looking as soon as we can."

"I understand, Sheriff. I can't tell you what a shock all this is. When I came here eight years ago, Seth had just completed his sophomore year at Purdue and was in his second summer on the staff here as a Junior Ranger. My wife and I always try to open our home to the boys, and I can tell you that Seth Clarke is the finest young man I ever met. We came to look on him as the son we never had. And when he and Sheila got married, they came here and stayed in one of the cabins for their honeymoon, or what they had of it before his emergency orders came. They've even come down a couple of times to have supper with us since he enrolled at the seminary. To tell you the truth, we were a little worried about them. It didn't seem that they were getting along too well. But we just can't believe all this . . ." He paused, his mind seemed to wander, unable to deal with the horror of the reality, his speech trailing off.

"Well, Mr. Hall, it looks like it happened," the sheriff said, "although I feel almost as bad about it as you do, and I never did meet the boy before we arrested him."

"What makes you think he might be at Turkey Run?" the Property Manager asked, getting back to business.

"This morning when we found that he had been back to his apartment at the school, we brought in some bloodhounds. Jerry Fuller over at Ladoga raises them, and we contract him on the rare occasions that we need any. So he brought over his dogs, and they followed Seth's trail across the highway to Eric Spritzker's place. Eric has the last house in town and owns two big pastures along Sugar Creek there. About a hundred yards down the creek, he has a boathouse. Says he don't know why he built it so far from the house. Anyway, he's a big fisherman, and he keeps a boat there with a thirty-five horse Mercury on it. Says his kids used to water ski when they were still at home. He also kept a canoe up in the rafters of the boathouse, a fifteen-foot Grumman aluminum one. Belonged to his boy. It was gone. Eric said he wouldn't have noticed it missing until the spring, if even then, if the dogs hadn't led us over there. But Seth could have known about the canoe, because just after he moved in over at the seminary he had asked Eric if he could fish on his property. Eric said he saw him over there two or three times. Said he was one of the best hands with a spinning rod he had ever seen. Anyway, knowing that he took his camping equipment, and knowing he was in the canoe, and knowing he used to work here, we thought this was the most likely place for him to head to, and we thought we had better come and take a look."

Lloyd Hall said that all made sense, but they had their work cut out for them if they were hoping to catch him at the park. When the sheriff asked why, he got up, and pointed to a large survey map of the park on the wall, and said, "The camp covers almost twenty-four hundred acres. I suppose all of you have visited here; almost everybody in this part of the state has. So you know that most of the park is limestone canyons, some of them pretty deep. Turkey Run is more like mountain terrain than anything in the Midwest, or at least in Indiana. About three to six million years ago, during the Ice Age, whenever the glacier melted, all of the boulders and other debris it had carried along with it were swept over this limestone here by the torrents created by the melting. That action ground out Sugar Creek and all the ravines and canyons around here. You can see more of it up at Shades State Park, too. Anyway, this terrain, together with all the trees and brush here, make more natural cover than you could find anywhere I know. If that boy is here and he wants to stay hidden, I bet he could do it till doomsday morning."

The State Police lieutenant said, "We hoped we could walk along the trails and see if anybody had been on them."

"Lord help you, that wouldn't do much good. We are open year round. Our lodge is booked solid most weekends all winter. Sometimes it's only with private individuals and families who want to get away a little, and other times it's groups that want a quiet, pretty place to have a meeting. We were full over the weekend and, cold though it was, a lot of people got out and walked around. I'll bet you won't find a foot of our most remote and rugged trails that somebody hasn't been over."

"What about food and water?" Horace asked. "Won't Seth have to come around the cabins or camping area for some of that?"

"Not a woodsman like him," Hall replied. "This clean snow can keep him in safe drinking water for quite a spell. And there's plenty of game around for anyone who knows where to look. As far as that goes, there are caves where he can get out of the cold and be almost as well protected against the weather as in a house, and nobody knows where those caves are better than him."

"Well," the sheriff said, "you make it sound awful discouraging. But we better get at it. I wonder if you and your staff could help us by taking each of us on one of those trails? You might notice things better than we would, since you know what it looks like normally at this time of year."

"Sure, Sheriff, I'll go along with you. My assistant can go with the lieutenant. Our naturalist can take your deputy, and our maintenance men can show the others around. We'll help you as conscientiously as we can. But I'll tell you, our hearts won't be in it. And Seth could lose any of us in these woods anytime he wanted. That's how he kept alive in Vietnam and got away from those Communists when he escaped. Not many have done that."

Three hours later, cold, wet, and exhausted, they all met back at the office. The Property Manager's prediction proved all too accurate. Now they would have to try the dogs, more men over a longer period of time, and helicopters.

The reason they didn't find evidence of Seth's arrival at Turkey Run at the time they searched was that his arrival hadn't yet occurred. By the time he had the canoe out of Spritzker's boathouse it was nearly five o'clock. Seth knew that farmers in the area got up early even in the winter, and anyone spotted riding in a canoe this time of year would attract attention. For that reason he pulled ashore when the sun started coming up. As he had expected, he'd gotten to the Shades by that time, and it was a simple matter of finding a ravine connecting to the creek, one in which trees grew thickly. It was unlikely that anyone would be out walking the trails on such a cold day, but he stayed in the canoe and did not permit himself to do any more than doze lightly; so that at any sound of danger he could paddle off quickly or do what he deemed necessary. After nightfall he would allow himself to fall into a deep sleep until three a.m., when he could be sure of moonlight and privacy in which to paddle the remaining fifteen miles.

At two p.m. sharp the Canon mounted the stairs at the front entrance of the Green Building. Reaching the landing where the stairs divided, he turned to the right, holding on to the seasoned and varnished sapling that was the bannister. Going down the hall, he was grateful for the recent benefactor who had underwritten the cost of stripping the pine walls of the dark varnish that had covered them for many years and replacing it with a lightly limed finish that showed the grain to better advantage and made the hall brighter and cheerier, less glaring. The new window at the end of the hall contributed measurably to this effect. On the next to the last door on his right, he found two narrow brass cardholders. One contained a fragment of a three-by-five card on which was typed "David Tharp" while the other contained a calling card with the name of Sebastian Seymour engraved in florid italic.

A voice started to call, "Come i . . . ," and then feet could be heard moving to the door. As it opened, the owner of the voice and feet said, "Come in, Father. I was studying and forgot for a moment that you were coming. That's why you got the usual bad manners we show around here. Here, I think the springs are more intact in this chair."

The sitting room was fifteen feet square. On the campus side were two dormer windows. Between them the sloping roofline came down to the mantle of a fireplace. It was obvious that the small study desks, their chairs, and two bookcases were seminary issue. The rest of the furnishings combined the results of inheritance from former student generations, Goodwill, and freight salvage purchases, and reflected the tastes, interests, and devotional habits of two very different young men. Above the desk on the left of the door was a large, complex, and intensely colored mandala. On the desk itself was an incense burner. A variety of candles, a clutter of pious objects students lumped under the rubric of "holy hardware," and books that ran toward Christian and more exotic devotional classics were the norm for that side of the room. On the other side, the main decoration was a Steppenwolf poster and another showing a giant gorilla above which was the caption, "If it feels good, do it!" The only explicitly religious symbol was a small, framed poster containing a rough drawing of Jesus, with a legend saying, "Wanted for Insurrection." Below the drawing, his crimes were listed along with a description of his appearance and associates. In the dormer on that side of the room was a large fish tank and a jumble of athletic equipment. The only books on the shelves were required texts.

Bothwell looked at his young host. Normally he did not visit the dormitory uninvited; he felt the students deserved to have a place where they were not under the eye of faculty, although he knew that some of his younger colleagues whose student days were very recent, and who were still perhaps uncertain as to which group to identify with, did drop by more often for a cup of coffee or a beer. David was only about five nine and had a slender build, but his agility made him Chase's obvious quarterback in annual touch football games with CTS in Indianapolis and Seabury-Western in Evanston, Illinois (the latter being the bloodier battle because it was intra-Episcopalian). Even though his dark brown hair was down to his blue chambray shirt collar and his moustache reminded Bothwell of Dr. Fu

Manchu, he had a well-scrubbed look that disqualified him from complete identification as a member of the Counterculture. He was too obviously one of the once born, too healthy minded to be weighed down with angst for himself or society. Yet he was a competent student, and he had a real commitment to working for a more equitable society.

"David," the Canon said, "I confess that I would not have assigned you and Mr. Seymour together to be roommates. You hardly seemed destined for anyone's Compatibility Award."

"No, Father, I don't guess we do. But my roomie last year was Drake Pearson, who graduated, so there was a vacancy in here. Anyway, until the last minute I thought that I was getting married after CPE last summer and didn't make arrangements to room with any of my friends, so I was willing to take whomever the business office assigned. But it hasn't worked out too badly. Not that Sebastian and I ever became best buddies or anything. Maybe the fact that we had so little in common kept the friction down. Truthfully, we hardly saw each other. Neither of us spent much time in the room. He slept some really weird hours, and I hate to be cooped up in a steamy room when I can be outdoors."

"Well, David, as I told you after class, I think the sheriff's department has been negligent in assuming that Seth killed Seymour and not checking out other possibilities. I have, therefore, decided to do a little looking around myself. The logical place to begin was where Mr. Seymour was on the evening before he died. Or, more to the point, in whose company he was."

"Wow, you're going to be Chase's answer to Father Brown in the Chesterton stories, aren't you? Sorry, Father, I don't mean to make light of what happened, but Sebastian never did seem very real to me, even as a roommate, and he seems even less so after all the weird things that have happened. All I really know is that he was planning to have dinner with someone in Indianapolis who had promised to drive him home. He didn't have a car, you know, and he was looking for a ride into the city at lunch on Friday, going from table to table asking if anyone was going in."

"Did he keep any sort of datebook?"

"Yes, he did, Father, but he kept it in what I called his purse. He had one of those pouches that he wore on a strap around his neck, but you couldn't see it because of that poncho he used to wear. I guess the sheriff got that after the autopsy."

"I suppose. But that reminds me, has the sheriff's department made any search of his room?"

"No, they haven't. Maybe they thought there wasn't any question about what happened, so that there wasn't anything they needed to find out here."

"I wonder if someone shouldn't pack up Mr. Seymour's things and deliver them to his parents?"

"Father, you're an old fox! As an amateur detective you don't have any right to search Sebastian's room, but as an official of the seminary, you would be performing a charitable act in looking after the property of the deceased."

"Young man, you must learn to hide this ability to see into the motives of others. Parishioners would find it frightening. I will get Frank to find some packing cases, and, if it's convenient with you, we will return shortly and pack up Mr. Seymour's belongings."

That evening after dinner Bothwell sat in his study amid the cardboard cartons in which the property of the deceased seminarian had been neatly packed. Nothing in the pockets of the clothing merited further investigation. He was not sure yet what to do with a small collection of packets and pill bottles they found tucked behind storage boxes on the shelf of the bedroom closet. After shaking the sitar to see if anything rattled around inside, he had left that in the car. Now he was methodically checking through papers and even lecture notes to see if any correspondence or doodling furnished leads. The address book found in the desk drawer had too many names to be immediately suggestive. Perhaps he would find something among the papers and through interviews he expected to have that would help him narrow down the list of acquaintances to be investigated. Meanwhile, it was interesting to see what Seymour had thought worth recording from the two lectures he had attended in Church History.

Katrina came in to tell him that he was wanted on the phone, and he picked up the receiver on his desk. "Hello, this is Roderick Bothwell."

"Hello, Canon, this is Sheila Clarke. I hate to bother you, but there's something I need some advice about. Could I come over for a few minutes? I promise I won't stay long."

"Certainly, Mrs. Clarke. Come right ahead. Or, if you prefer, I will come to your place."

"No, I'll be right there. Thank you. Goodbye."

Wondering what this was about, the Canon stood and buttoned the ancient wine-colored smoking jacket that he had long worn over his rabat vest and collar when he spent the evening at this desk. His neat burgundy calf slippers fitted too well to flop as he walked toward the front door. The young woman had sounded upset, and she did not need the formal reception used by Katrina to greet unannounced female callers.

Taking Sheila's sheepskin coat to hang up, Bothwell noticed she wore jeans and a University of Illinois sweatshirt that looked like it had been worn to paint in. Leading her into the parlor and seating her in front of the healthy fire in a big wingchair, he asked if he could get her a cup of coffee or a glass of port.

"No, Canon, I didn't come to stay, I just wanted to get your advice. It has to do with all the reporters. Since the news broke, they haven't let me alone. When I came out this morning to go to work, they were waiting by the car. When I went to the cafeteria at the office, they were there. They were waiting in the parking lot when I got off work. They were in front of the apartment when I drove up. They have been on the phone all day. They won't believe me when I tell them I have nothing to say to them."

"That must be very distressing. Still, I can see their point. This has to be one of the biggest stories to come their way for some time. Beauty queen, war hero, sex, drugs, religion, and violence. Their readers and viewers would lap it up."

"Canon, they remind me of those leeches that Seth told me were such a problem for prisoners in Vietnam. They live on other people's blood, and if you try to brush them off, they will leave their suckers inside to infect you."

"Have you always felt this way about them?"

"No, and I suppose that's a lot of the trouble. Before, when I was in the pageant and later when we got married, I loved it and felt that getting to know so many reporters on a first-name basis made me quite a celebrity. But now it seems so ghoulish."

"What harm do you think it would do to talk with them?"

"I have asked myself the same question, and I'm not sure. I guess that, while I am still convinced that Seth killed Sebastian, some important principle is involved in my not being a party in helping other people think so. It's all very confusing, but that's as close to it as I can get. Also related to that is my feeling that if anyone is guilty of Sebastian's death, it's me."

"I see. Would it help to move over here into one of my guestrooms for a while? I am sure that Katrina would take very good care of you."

"Thank you, Canon. I've thought about moving in with one of the other couples down in the Hutches, but it doesn't seem right. It seems to me that I ought to stay in our apartment now."

"I'll tell you what, then. I'll ask some of the other student husbands to make a point of being around at the times you leave and get home every day. They ought to be able to discourage too much aggressiveness from the reporters. And I'm sure that as soon as they learn that you are not going to tell them anything, and as other stories break and call them away, they'll soon get tired of hanging around in the cold waiting for you."

# 11

Seth lay on his cot in his hut in the camp they had ironically nicknamed Palm Springs. He tried to shift his ankles to a less painful position in the stocks, but they had been clamped on so tight that any movement meant only that new skin would be abraded off his leg. That, added to mosquito bites, boils, and fungus infection, was all he needed. The bar on which the arm stocks were attached was under his back at the bottom of the shoulder blades and, besides making its own indentation in his flesh, it placed a strain on all the muscles in his upper back and neck. The cramp after a night's exhausted but fitful sleep he knew to be endurable only from experience. The guards had not even brought him his morning's ration of rice. In his condition it would make him gag, but he would force it down, even if he vomited a couple of times over the first mouthfuls. Maybe today they would at least give him enough water to cover the bottom of the cup.

Even more than he longed for food, he yearned to be let out of the stocks long enough to run down the log walkway to the primitive latrine, hoping that he would make it in time. The dysentery was returning, and his gut had already convulsed several times since he had awakened. It was only a matter of time before he would no longer be able to contain the diarrheic flow, and his thin black cotton pajamas would again be stuck to his body and the loathsome smell would return.

He would not be able to continue his resistance much longer. Four Eyes, the cadre, had been so angry when he read the last exercise Seth had written to show what he had learned from his instruction about the great kindness of the Front to its prisoners. It was true, of course, that the Geneva convention was not being observed, but its provisions were for prisoners of war, not criminals arrested in the invasion of a land whose peace-loving people were engaged in a struggle for self-determination. In the circumstances the Front was being extraordinarily generous in protecting the captured criminals from the righteous wrath of the Vietnamese people and even providing food and shelter for them when their people were badly in need of such commodities themselves. How could he have been so ungrateful as not to acknowledge his crimes and to state how well he was being looked after? Why did he fill the five sheets of paper given to him with his name, rank, and serial number, repeated endlessly in tiny handwriting that filled not only the lines but the margins of the paper as well?

Suddenly the explanation of the delay in his morning's rice became clear to him. Beyond the buzz of the mosquitoes there was an extraordinary stillness to the camp. Now a hum that he had thought was part of the mosquito sound began to stand out as a louder thumping noise. It was growing louder and more distinct. A chopper was coming their way. Yesterday the gooks had laughed because a little Cessna Bird Dog had flitted over several times looking like its civilian light plane cousin with its propeller and large upper wing. The VC's knew from experience that it was unarmed, and so they laughed at it, even firing a few 7.62 mm. rounds at it from their Type 56-1 assault rifles. Mussolini, as the prisoners called a fat bully among the guards, had come over to tell him what a sophisticated air defense system they had, thanks to the technology of their freedom-loving allies in Russia and China, a statement Seth knew was not just propaganda but literal truth. They did not realize that the Cessna 01-E spent its time looking for targets. The sound he heard now was undoubtedly one of the several Hueys that would descend and fire into the camp somewhere between fifty and seventy-five rockets apiece.

The bitter irony was that it was impossible to tell from the air what was a small camp holding American prisoners and what was a station along this outlet of the Ho Chi Minh Trail supply route. The enemy must have heard the helicopter and gone into the jungle. Now the Huey would be coming in and firing its rockets into the hootches, and the only human targets in them would be American servicemen locked helplessly onto their cots for their unwillingness to speak disloyally of their country. The chopper was getting closer now, it would begin to fire any minute. In frustration and fear and rage, Seth began to scream.

The sound of his own voice awakened him, and for a minute it was hard for him to get oriented. The cave was dark this far back. He recognized that the ache and strain on his back and arms came from his backpack, which he had been too tired to pull himself out of when he had finally reached the cave early that morning. He had stumbled over a rock, fallen, tried to stand, got as far as a sitting position, and then fallen backwards onto his pack. In that cramped position he had slept what must have been only three or four hours. The roar of the chopper continued in his ears, and he shook his head to clear out the sound. It would not go away, but instead became more distinct. It was not a Huey, it was too small for that. It was more like a Cayuse. The choppers the State Police used to spot speeders must have been brought in to search for him. That meant they had a pretty good idea he was in Turkey Run.

Frank let his employer out of the Packard at the rear entrance of the old administration building at Wabash and went to search for a parking place. As the Canon went in the tall double doors and turned down the hall, he could not help thinking that Lew Wallace had walked down the same hall when it was new and he was writing *Ben Hur*. Looking back on it, *Ben Hur* was probably one of the early influences that had led Bothwell eventually to the study of Church History. Coming to the office of the Dean of Students, he was told by the secretary that he was expected. The high ceilings of the office and its large windows gave a sense of grace and dignity to the room that was enhanced by the Williamsburg style of its decor, the well-filled bookcases, and the sunny paintings that decorated the walls.

The Canon and the Dean were old friends through St. John's Church, so they shook hands warmly before Bothwell's coat was taken by the Dean. After he walked back to the Princeton chair behind the desk and removed the fat cigar from between his teeth, the Dean said, "Well, Rod, my secretary told me that you had called and asked for an appointment. What brings you to these secular corridors? Are you trying to sow seeds of faith in this unlikely soil?"

"No, Vincent, as worth doing as that would be, I am here on a different errand. You have undoubtedly heard with the rest of the nation that one of our students is suspected of murder. I am of the opinion that the sheriff's department has been delinquent in not investigating other possibilities. It would have been entirely out of character for Mr. Clarke to commit the crime. Since the police have not looked into other possible explanations, I have decided to do so myself."

The Dean chuckled. "If I remember correctly, Collingwood compared the work of a historian to that of a fictional detective, but I have never known one before who tried to live out that role model."

"Several people have made that comparison, but I assure you that I am not engaged in this investigation for entertainment. The ministry, not to say the life, of a very fine young man is at stake here, and I mean to do what I can to safeguard the contribution he can make to the church."

"I knew you were serious, Rod, and I shouldn't have teased you. What can I do to help?"

"We have reason to believe that the young man who died was somehow involved in narcotics, not just as a casual user, but as someone who expected to supply at least a few other people. I delicately asked one of our more responsible students where any seminarian who might consider purchasing some marijuana would go to find it, assuring him that I was not snooping into student behavior, but rather looking into possible unsavory connections that Mr. Seymour may have had. The student told me that he thought this campus the most likely place to make a contact. I'm still not trying to uncover drug traffic as such, and I certainly would not be party to any effort to give Wabash any unfavorable publicity. I wonder, therefore, if you could tell me in utter confidence something about the drug situation here at the college?"

The Dean of Students moved back his chair, pulled out the lower right-hand desk drawer, propped his feet on it and folded his hands across his ample mid-section.

"Now you've asked the dirty one, Rod. The official answer is that there is none. Six years ago that would not only have been the answer, it would have been true. It's hard to look at the kids on the campus today, with their long hair, beards, and surplus-store-closeout wardrobes, and remember that in 1964 the students on this campus rooted for Goldwater.

"You know what our students are like, Rod. In a sense, they are as culturally deprived as any ghetto kid in Chicago. They are very bright, or they would never make it through our selective admissions screening. And most of them have to be pretty well off, or their parents couldn't pick up the tab.

"But in spite of all our efforts to cast our recruiting net wider, the majority of those who matriculate for the first time every fall are from professional families in the county seats of Indiana. Most of them had never listened to classical music, looked at paintings, read poems, or even gone to plays or read serious novels before they arrived here. There's a whole new world here just waiting to activate those minds. It's a heady experience for them. One of the first effects of all this on them is to make them despise where they came from. That doesn't mean that after six or seven years when they have completed their professional training, they won't go right back to those same towns and hang out a shingle with their old man, but at first a lot of rejection goes on, what used to be called kicking over the traces."

The Dean paused to relight his cigar, took a deep draw, and then continued, "The peace movement has provided them an outlet. That doesn't mean that I am opposed to the movement. I do a lot of draft counseling out of this office. But I see clearer than they do, perhaps, that a complex of motives gets mixed in. The movement allows them to revolt against their parents while feeling morally superior at the same time. The drugs are as exciting to them as war was to earlier generations, and they carry with them an air that you would probably call Gnostic.

"What I hope this office can do is to see that they have a safe island on which to do mild experimentation. A little pot or a few pills, and we don't make too much fuss and nothing ever goes beyond campus security. But the minute that we hear about acid, or speed, or especially horse, we come down like a ton of bricks. Faculty members are on the lookout for telltale signs, and even the frat presidents alert me to potential problems."

The Dean stopped, obviously in thought. Then he said to Bothwell, "Now, I could make some damn good guesses about who on campus might be doing a little dealing, but that probably wouldn't get you to the level you want to go. I think their supplier is a guy named Grover Riley, who lives in a trailer out on Route 32. Wouldn't you know, he's a DePauw dropout."

The Dean got to his feet. "Enough business. Come on over to the Scarlet Inn, and let me buy you a cup of coffee. It's been a long time since you came by to elevate the conversation."

The Canon rose and walked toward his coat. "No, Vince, I thank you more than I can say for your frankness. I assure you I will not compromise the information that you have given me. But I must get back to New Charleston and look like a professional professor instead of an amateur detective, or I'll begin to hear from a Dean who is very different from you."

Back in his study that evening, the Canon completed his preparation for the next day's classes, including the marking of reading reports submitted by the Juniors. He had started examining Sebastian's papers when Katrina knocked on his door and said that a student had come to see him. The student was Michael Idriss, a quiet Middler who kept to himself, but had met all his obligations with promptness and some flair until recently. As the year developed, the faculty began to have some concern over him. He appeared to be having a worse case of Middler slump than most of his classmates and, while he was normally a few pounds overweight, flesh had dropped off him to the point that he now looked unhealthy. The severe weight loss combined with a sad, preoccupied expression that had become his habitual demeanor led his professors who were psychologically oriented to conclude that he was undergoing a serious siege of depression. That interpretation certainly tallied with the decreased quality of his work and a decline in his attendance of Morning Prayer and the Eucharist at the beginning of each day.

When Bothwell had him seated and the offer of refreshment refused, he turned his full gaze on him and confirmed the impression he had formed when Idriss had come in the door: he was white as a sheet and seemed very emotional. "Mr. Idriss," he said, "you appear very distressed. If there is anything I can do to help, I would consider it a privilege."

"Father, I came because I might be of some help to you. Is it true that you are investigating the death of Sebastian Seymour?"

"Yes, I am. Do you have some information that may be relevant."

"I may. I hope so, because I certainly wouldn't discuss this if I didn't have to. My conscience would give me no peace until I talked to you. Father, I hope what I have to say won't go any further unless absolutely necessary."

"That promise is hard to make when I don't know what it covers, but if I can keep what you say confidential without violating my other obligations, I will do so. You know that faculty are not allowed to hear the confessions of students precisely because of the seal. In the distant past an unscrupulous student confessed to each member of the faculty in hopes that the seal of the confessional would not allow them to vote for his dismissal. He was not as clever as he thought, however, because the evidence on which his dismissal was based had been known to them previously and through other channels. But, I stray from the point."

"No, you're closer to it than you think. I don't have any unconfessed actual sins to tell you about, only information I hope will not become common knowledge even among the faculty. Father, my sexual orientation is toward members of my own sex. I know that many homosexuals say that their condition has never been for them a cause for shame or guilt feelings, but I have always despised myself for it, and part of what my conversion to serious Christianity meant to me was getting that compulsive behavior off my back. I felt that I had been let out of prison. I don't mean anything miraculous. My orientation was not changed, but somehow I did not feel tempted anymore. I had been chaste five years before I asked the bishop to admit me as a postulant."

"Well, Mr. Idriss, I find your story deeply moving and can say that I think you are certainly to be admired for your attitude, but I'm not sure that I see the bearing of this on Mr. Seymour's death."

"It's just this, Father. I was in the habit of taking my shower at odd times during the day rather than to expose myself to too much stimulation in the bathroom. I didn't want to push my luck. Anyway, Sebastian must have caught on to my secret, because whenever I went down to the showers he would come along shortly afterwards. As I said, no one else was generally around at that time. He would never say anything to me, but he would come down and take off his bathrobe and go about his ablutions in the nude. I always averted my eyes as well I could, but he seemed to know why I did and to take some pleasure in it. Later I would remember what I had seen. He had a very beautiful body in an ethereal way, and the sight of it would keep creeping back into my imagination. I became so aroused a few times that I even masturbated, something I had not done for years. Then I began to despair of my ability ever to be continent, and my dreams of effective priesthood began to fade. I have been miserable ever since he got here . . . but I didn't come down here to tell you my troubles. I thought this insight into Sebastian's character might be useful to you in your investigation."

"Michael, thank you for this courageous action. I am sure that you will be a wonderful priest. Don't worry, none of us can live up to his own standards of what a priest should be. Yet God is able to use whatever feeble gifts we offer. Even St. Paul learned to see it was in his weakness that God's grace was most evident. But what you told me could be immensely important. It makes sense of other things I had begun to learn and should simplify my job enormously. Back to you—are you okay now?"

"Do you know, Father, I haven't felt so good for ages." He stood up and smiled. "Talking to you has lifted an enormous weight from my shoulders. I want to go down to the chapel now. I have some catching up to do."

# 12

The area of Indianapolis into which Frank drove the Canon had once been solid middle-class territory, which could be seen from the large two-story frame houses that lined the street, ornate with towers, turrets, gables, and gingerbread. Now these had all been turned into cheap boarding houses or multi-family dwellings. Batteries of doorbells stood under multiple mailboxes on some porches, while others had been enclosed to provide space for a few more tenants so that volume of business could offset the low per-unit profit.

The church building which was their destination still had "Fourth Christian Church" lettered in the stone tablet above the main entrance, although the large painted sign on the lawn proclaimed it to be "Brotherhood Church." It was something of an architectural monument, being the only surviving edifice in the city built on the Akron plan, which put the pulpit in the corner and had pews fanning out from it on an inclined auditorium floor that required every eye in the building to be focused on the preacher.

Bothwell remembered being there once when the Episcopal Society for Cultural and Racial Unity of which he was a member had cooperated with other agencies in the metropolitan area for a march in support of open housing. At that time there had been huge banners inside bearing such scripture verses as "God hath made of one blood all nations of men for to dwell on all the face of the earth" and "God hath shewed me that I should not call any man common or unclean."

The design of the church auditorium, he recalled, would not have been necessary for the Reverend Bob Smith. His piercing eye would have drawn the gaze of all, however they had been seated. There had been something eclectic as well as electric about his oratory. Bothwell recognized the rhetorical style of the tent revivalists in small Mississippi towns when he was a boy, a style very similar to that of radio evangelists who broadcasted late at night from Del Rio, Texas. Also present was something of the hypnotic power of Adolph Hitler. And, not surprising in the ghetto, something of the glorious homiletical tradition of the black church appeared, in which poetry materialized so often in the midst of a congregation. Even then it had not been too clear what point Smith might be making, but one knew that it was important, and that one wanted to be a part of whatever he was advocating. Bothwell had thought about Ben Franklin's response to the preaching of George Whitefield.

Today he went to the church office in the Educational Building behind the church. Instead of the dark, dirty-looking red brick of which the church was constructed, this building was made of tile blocks ranging in shade from dark rust to deep purple. The architectural style was an indeterminate modern from the late thirties that incorporated glass brick wherever possible. Going through the door, Bothwell noticed heavy chains wrapped around the opener bar on the inside, suggesting that security could be made very tight. The low-wattage lights along the corridor revealed little more than that the paint job on the walls was amateur, and the hall carpet was threadbare. Arriving at an island of light midway down the corridor, he discovered a large window let into the wall with a ledge about hip high.

Through the window he could see an outer office with two large steel desks at the far side, one on each side of a varnished door with a frosted glass window showing the painted words "Assistant Pastor." On the corridor side of the room the ledge at the bottom of the window was extended into the room to make a built-in reception desk. In the window glass were two holes, a round one two feet up from the ledge through which one could speak, and a semicircular one opening a few inches over the ledge through which things could be slipped. Young women were seated at the desks; one of them was black and the other white, but otherwise they appeared much alike. They both wore clothing ten years out of style. The skirts were long, but the tops of the dresses were tight around generous, well-shaped breasts. Neither girl wore any makeup, but both had elaborate hairdos. A slim, blond man in his early twenties sat on top of one of the desks, talking to one young woman. His manner was earnest, and his attire was what Bothwell could only think of as "square," although he had never before used that word in its current popular meaning. In the doorway to the corridor side of the desk on the left stood a tall, immobile, powerfully built young man in trousers and shirt of olive drab wool with his pants legs tucked into puttees. He wore a maroon beret, and he stood at parade rest.

At first the group in the office seemed oblivious to Bothwell's presence, but when he rapped on the glass and said, "Excuse me," the white girl got up, showing an annoyed expression, and walked to the glass, resting her knuckles on the ledge and leaning toward the speaking hole. "What do you want?" she asked.

"I am Professor Roderick Bothwell from Chase Clergy Training College. I have met the Reverend Mr. Smith at several civil rights meetings, and I would like to speak with him about one of our recent students who was formerly associated with this church."

Without a word to Bothwell, the girl turned around and walked back to her desk where she stooped in whispered conversation with the white man. He came to the window and presented to Bothwell a face that lacked any expression. "About whom do you wish to inquire?"

"Mr. Sebastian Seymour."

"That name is unknown here."

"But, sir, I know that he was the Reverend Mr. Smith's assistant for some time. He must be known here. Would you please at least send in my card to Mr. Smith and inform him that I would like a minute of his time?"

The voice continued to speak with no emotion and an irreducible amount of inflection. "Our leader has many grave responsibilities, and it is our duty to see that he is undistracted. I will have to ask you to leave."

When Bothwell seemed to hesitate about fulfilling the request, the young man, without looking back, raised his right arm in a beckoning gesture. The black man began to walk toward the window.

Pulling himself up to his full height, Bothwell replaced his homburg on his head, saying, "Then I'll not presume further upon your good nature, sir," and, bowing slightly, he said, "Ladies," and turned and walked back to the entrance with dignity and an absence of haste.

It was only a short drive from Brotherhood Church to All Saints, the major Episcopal presence in the inner city of Indianapolis. A grandmotherly black woman looked after the phones, showed visitors to whatever agency they wished to visit, and did what typing the Rector did not bang out on his old upright Underwood with open sides. Seeing the Canon, her face was wreathed in a wide smile as she said, "Hello, Dr. Bothwell. Father O'Grady will be delightfully surprised to see you. You know your way back."

Going down the hall, he came to the open door of the Rector's study and stood at the entrance. The Rev. James Mitchell O'Grady looked up from a desk that was a mound of assorted books and papers, and then he stood to stretch out a hand to welcome his visitor. "Rod, you old curmudgeon, what brings you out of your ivory tower? Are you slumming in the big city or merely trying to get away from the Dean? Whatever the explanation, sit down, and let me pour you a cup of coffee. I suppose it's too early in the day for anything else, even for a couple of old sinners like us."

The Canon looked with affection at the priest in front of him, who could have inspired the popular song of a number of years back, "Mr. Five by Five." His black suit coat was thrown over the back of the chair, and he sat at the desk in his rabat vest and white clerical shirt. The large room seemed to reflect his expansive personality, being wide, disorderly, and yet bearing an air of dedication and serviceability. The shelves were packed with thick books, ranging from a technical theological collection to the latest works in psychology and sociology. A plaster Mexican crucifix stood on top of one bookshelf, a leather-bound missal was on top of another, and an illuminated page from a fifteenth-century antiphonary hung in a wide black frame on the wall.

"Hello, Jamie, it's good to see you," said the Canon, returning the warm handclasp. "I take my coffee black, as you know. I wish this were only a social visit, because we see far too little of one another, considering how relatively near we live. But both of us are such compulsive workers that we do not follow the ghostly counsel we give to others about recreation being a necessary ingredient in the Christian's rule of life."

"I knew it was too much to expect that you had come by only for the pleasure of my company. But I'll bear up under the blow bravely. What can I help you with, old friend?"

"I want information connected with our recently deceased student, Mr. Seymour, about whom you have undoubtedly read in the press. I am convinced that our Mr. Clarke could not have killed him, and I am trying to uncover other possibilities. First, as I recall, you were against his being approved by the Commission on Ministry in the diocese. If you can do so without violating confidences, I would like you to tell me your reasons for that stand. Then, secondly, as you also know, before his conversion to Anglicanism, Mr. Seymour was associated with the Brotherhood Church. I visited there earlier today and had an unsatisfactory interview. I would like your considered opinion on that operation."

"Glad to help you with both questions, Rod. The reasons for the attempt to blackball came from what I had heard in the community here. I could go into detail, but it all boils down to realizing that our boy had no real commitment to social justice or the needs of the poor, but that he was an operator out to build a power base among those he was supposed to be helping.

"Which makes him very much like his erstwhile employer, with one major exception. From all I can tell, Seymour was completely cynical. Bob Smith, on the other hand, has a real Messiah complex. I am sure that if we could sit him down in Episcopal Community Services up the hall and give him a complete battery of psychological examinations, we would have a certifiable paranoiac on our hands, with a fully developed alternative reality system. He knows who the enemies are, and he was appointed by God to save his people from them.

"Up until recently his method of 'saving' was to tell his people the truth about their enemies and to organize them against them, but I think that now has changed. It must have begun about the time that Sebastian left, which hurt Smith badly. And then there were a few other defectors, some of whom were pretty disillusioned and threatening to blow the whistle to the denominational authorities. He began using his Soldiers of Christ to keep discipline in his protest marches. It was a high morale unit almost like a crack ROTC drill team, and they even had uniformed girl sponsors who gave a cheerleader enthusiasm to the whole business. Lately I've heard that they are taking lessons in unarmed combat at meetings, and also that they have been studying what Che, Mao, Ho, and Giap have written about guerilla warfare. There are also stories about accidents happening to apostates, and a couple of ex-members of the Brotherhood have gone missing. All of this is pretty vague, but I think you can assume that it gives you an accurate assessment of reality."

At first Frank drove past Grover Riley's trailer on the Lebanon road into Crawfordsville and had gone some way into town from where he had got off the Interstate from Indianapolis before he decided that he had better turn around and look again. Heading back out of town, he saw the trailer, although it was well back from the road and obscured by a thick row of poplars planted along the highway, looking very much like the windbreaks planted by Wisconsin farmers to prevent snowdrifts. Turning into the well-traveled driveway, he brought the Packard to rest beside an ornately painted high-wheel pickup with a camper body. There was also a Pontiac Firebird, black with painted flames all over the hood and fenders and mud splashes taking up where the paint left off, parked in front of the trailer.

Even before the Canon opened the back door of the big limousine, he could hear—or, at any rate, feel—the shock waves of what he took to be music, although his bachelor state, his disinterest in popular amusements, and his isolation from the living quarters of students had spared him up until that time from much assault on his ears by hard rock. Nor had he had occasion to visit what is euphemistically called a mobile home before, although he had been aware for some time that these relatively low-cost dwellings had become a progressively more familiar sight along the highways of the country.

It took several knocks to be heard above the din, but eventually the door was opened by a young woman who found Bothwell's appearance as bizarre as he found hers. Though she was of medium height, her breasts were abnormally large for her thin body. There could be no doubt about their size or their authenticity since she wore a gauze Turkish blouse knotted under them. The material was translucent enough to be embarrassing to the Canon. When his eyes attempted to stray, they found no relief. Going down, he first saw an amazingly wide expanse of skin at the midriff above jeans that hugged her hips so low that the absence of visible pubic hair was the only evidence Bothwell saw that the young woman practiced any toilette. The most amazing aspect of her appearance to him was the red and blue wing of a tattooed butterfly peeping out of the top of her jeans about where someone else's appendectomy scar might be.

It was when he looked at her face that Bothwell was most distressed by the girl's appearance. To begin with, he had never before seen a blond Afro on a white person. Her complexion was pimply and grainy, as though she did not wash but also was indicative of something more. Her unpainted lips hung loose. But it was her eyes that most distressed the priest. Set back in painted pits, they looked unfocused and a little glazed. "Child," he thought, "our Savior died on the cross to save us from meaningless lives. How has his influence made no mark on you?" As moved by her as he would be by a lost child, he offered up a silent prayer.

Making some effort to take in what she was seeing, the girl giggled and said, "Boy, have you got the wrong house," and turned back into the trailer.

"God damn it, Sibyl, who the hell's at the door?" The yell was followed by a face seeking to answer its own question. Before Bothwell stood a man in his twenties whose face looked older and harder. He was not tall, but he was as well muscled as an oil field roustabout. Bothwell thought the man looked to be from the redneck gene bank because his features were reminiscent of the entire white population of the north Mississippi town where the Canon had grown up. In his cowboy shirt and tight jeans, he could easily have been a "Coveite" from around Sewanee, except for his long hair. Even that, however, did not really belong with the rest of his appearance, but instead looked almost put on for a part in a play.

Seeing the clerical collar, he said, "We don't want any, Mister." His accent reminded Bothwell that a friend had once described that section of Indiana as "the northern part of the south."

"Mr. Riley, I am Canon Bothwell from the Clergy Training College. I need to ask you some questions in relation to the recent death of one of our students, Mr. Sebastian Seymour."

"That's tough on you, buddy. I don't need to answer no questions." The veneer of DePauw had entirely rubbed off.

As he started to close the door he was interrupted both by the Canon's galoshed foot against the metal frame and the authority of the voice. "Mr. Riley, I am doing some research on the driving habits of the citizens of Montgomery County, and I had thought of stationing my driver on the highway right-of-way out here to take down the license numbers of every car going into this drive, using binoculars often to make certain of accuracy."

"I would call the cops and have him taken in for harassment."

"Yes, and I could have him replaced with a succession of seminarians. Of course, the police could station someone in the drive to arrest them as they came on duty, if you would like a squad car parked on your property."

Riley stared hard at Bothwell for a moment, then stepped back.

"Come on in. What kind of questions did you want to ask?"

"Thank you for your hospitality," said the Canon as he entered the door. He sat down on a built-in sofa upholstered in a garish plaid fabric that may have been improved in its appearance by several cigarette burns and rips through which gray cotton stuffing was emerging. The room reminded him of a sailboat in its compactness, but its sloppiness was where the similarity ended.

"We know that Mr. Seymour purchased at least some narcotics for his personal use and may have begun to purchase larger quantities for the use of others. I, of course, would not ask you to incriminate yourself, and I can assure you that I am not engaged in trying to put an end to the local drug traffic, as desirable as I think that might be. But I wonder if you can tell me if Mr. Seymour obtained his controlled substances locally."

"Naw. I admit that I've heard of the guy, but he didn't do any business in town. I've heard that he had contacts in the nigger section of Indianapolis. I can't give you any names, and I wouldn't if I could. Those mothers play rough."

"Thank you, Mr. Riley, and good day." Rising again and leaving, the Canon was relieved to have the door shut on the grating noise as he turned back to his car.

# 13

When the Canon entered the chapel for Evensong that day, he noticed Sheila kneeling in the court of the gentiles. She was still there when the office was over. After he had hung up his gown and put on his overcoat, hat, and gloves, he waited for her in the narthex where all of the faculty and students had coat pegs at which they could exchange outer garments for academic gowns, or vice versa. This change of clothing as a transition from the profane sphere to the sacred and back again had long caused Bothwell to regard this vestibule as a decompression chamber such as ocean divers stopped in while going into or out of the depths. He stood for ten minutes, seeing no one but the sacristan who had straightened up after the service and Pete Whiston, the charismatic fiddler, who must have remained in the ecstatic trance he had fallen into during the vesper service. Finally, Bothwell heard soft steps coming down the aisle and saw the swinging doors open.

"Mrs. Clarke." He spoke softly because she still seemed to be very much preoccupied, and he did not wish to startle her. "I hope you don't mind. I saw you in chapel and thought I'd wait and walk down campus with you and find out how you are."

As she looked up, her solemn face broke into a soft smile and she said, "That's very kind of you, Canon. I hope that my slowness has not kept you from anything."

"No, my time has been well spent. My thoughts have been so busy lately that standing quietly for a few minutes has been a blessed relief. You're too young to remember who Harry Hopkins was, but he was a busy man who said that a change of troubles can be as good as a vacation. But tell me, how have you been?"

"It's been very strange, Canon," Sheila said as Bothwell held open the door for her, and they started down the steps. "I gave Seth a very hard time when he was with me, but now that he's gone, I worry about him constantly. It's like when he was a POW. I hadn't prayed much before, but then I kept asking God to watch over him and take care of him and bring him back safely to me. What I did when he returned is another story, but that's the way I was when he was gone. And now I'm living that experience all over again. I know you aren't supposed to bargain with God, but I keep promising that if only Seth comes back to me once more, this time I really will treat him right. Canon, what's going to happen to him?"

"We can't be sure, my dear. I have great confidence in his ability to elude the law officers looking for him just as he avoided capture when he escaped from the Viet Cong. I also believe he can be exonerated if we have enough time to put together the evidence in his defense. My biggest concern now is that he may try to leave this part of the country and establish another identity elsewhere so that we would lose our capacity for contact with him."

"Do you know how to get in touch with him?" The young woman's eyes were brilliant with expectation.

"I think I do, but I also believe it would be very dangerous to try until we are much further along in our efforts to prove his innocence." When he saw her crushed expression, Bothwell said, "Mrs. Clarke, my housekeeper has the evening off, and I had planned on driving over to the Red Barn to eat some of their good fried chicken. I would be honored if you would join me."

Momentarily her face was lit by a radiant smile. "You really know how to get a girl, Canon. To tell you the truth, I have been dreading going home to that empty apartment. As often as I made Seth eat alone, I can't bear the idea of doing it myself now."

When Bothwell said something about getting out the big old Packard, mentioning that his driver was also off for the evening, Sheila insisted that she drive. After they had settled into the Clarke's Squareback and were humming along in the direction of the restaurant, the Canon commented that he felt a little guilty about having two other human beings devote their lives to his convenience. Certainly not many clergy could afford a domestic staff, even if they would care to have one, but he had been left comfortably well off by his parents.

Arriving as a brand-new PhD at the Clergy Training College twenty-two years earlier, he had originally taken all his meals at the refectory, but after a year he realized the starchy menu, an institutional necessity where young men are fed, was doing terrible things to a sedentary body already inclined to flesh. Katrina had come to him then after Frank had left their farm to serve in the Army during the Korean War. He volunteered three months before reaching the upper age limit. When Frank returned in the fall of 1953, he was on disability for a leg lost to a land mine. While his prosthesis was good enough for him to return to farming, he decided to help around the house until the right place came on the market. But it seemed so natural for Frank and Katrina to live with the Canon that they stayed on.

"They certainly have brought order and convenience into my life and are the nearest thing to a family I have. I hope I haven't deprived them of greater fulfillment in another line of endeavor," the Canon said in conclusion to this account of his domestic arrangements.

Over their pre-prandial glass of wine, their crisply fried chicken, and finally their chess pie and coffee, the Canon told Sheila about his efforts to discover who beyond Seth might have had a reason for wishing Sebastian dead. She was surprised at the length of the list and admitted she had certainly been mistaken in her judgment about him, something she had already begun to realize before that evening.

After Bothwell paid the check and they bundled up to go to the car, Sheila became subdued and hardly said a word during the first few miles of the trip back to the seminary. There were few other cars on the road, and the darkness of the night before the moon rose gave the two of them a deep sense of aloneness together, as though they were on a tiny island in the sea of the night. The Volkswagen heater intensified that atmosphere by its failure to overcome all the chill of the January night.

Finally Sheila spoke, reluctantly at first, as if she had at last gotten the courage to share what was on her mind. "Canon, I want to ask you something that may seem off the subject and, worse, it's going to make me sound very conceited, but I wouldn't ask if I didn't think it was very important to my ability to make Seth a good wife, if he ever gets through all of this and wants to come back to me."

"Go right ahead, my dear. I will answer you as well as I can."

"Canon, your reaction to me has been different from that of almost everyone I've ever known. I don't mean only boys after I was mature enough for them to be interested in me—I mean everybody, beginning with my parents and extending to my teachers after I started school. They didn't treat me the way they treated everyone else. Even adults seemed—how shall I put it?— deferential to me. I was always teacher's pet and given a lot of privileges and generally got away with murder. I don't know why the other kids didn't hate me. They didn't particularly like me, but they seemed to feel it was okay for me to be treated differently."

She paused, glancing sideways at the Canon, while still watching the road ahead. "But you don't treat me that way. You treat me like you treat anyone else. Or maybe even more critically, because there have been times when you were looking at me like you'd seen a snake or something. Yet I don't get the feeling that you are indifferent to beauty, or that you don't find women attractive. Please forgive my frankness, but your answer could help me to change my life."

Bothwell suppressed a smile. "Well, my dear, first let me say that I had no idea I was so transparent. I do hope that I have never given offense. But let me also say that I can believe that your perceptions are accurate. I can easily imagine that you have been treated in an exceptional way because of what I do not hesitate to call your beauty, although it is a term I use sparingly. As to my apparent invulnerability, I learned the hard way. When I was an undergraduate as Sewanee, I had what in those days was called an understanding with a very fine girl from my hometown. She and I had grown up together, and I suppose I had always taken her for granted. The quickness of her mind, her maturity of character, her real loveliness of face and figure, and her affection for me I accepted as the ordinary facts of everyday life."

Bothwell closed his eyes briefly, as if looking into the past within.

"My fraternity always had a big ball on the weekend nearest General Lee's birthday, and we invited our dates up for the festivities. One year a fraternity brother invited a young woman from Nashville. Although she was blond where you are a brunette, she was as spectacular as you. Like every other man on the mountain, I was smitten. I'm afraid I paid little attention to my sweetheart while she was there. Amazing to me at the time, the boy who had invited the Nashville girl over was almost the only one of the fraternity men not in love with her. He indicated to me that I would not be cutting in on his territory if I pursued her after she returned home. To make a long story short, I did and was successful. I was engaged to her for two years before it gradually began to dawn on me that except for her looks, she was a very ordinary person. She was not nearly so interesting to be with as the girl from home that I had thrown over for her.

"She was already beginning to get bored with me, because there was nothing dashing or glamorous about me. At any rate, she returned my ring with very little sign of heartbreak. By that time, I had received an invitation to the wedding of the only girl I have ever thought I could be truly happy with, and so I have lived out my life in loneliness."

Sheila glanced again at the Canon, her eyes brimming with sympathy. He cleared his throat and continued. "Having once noted that spectacular beauty is not necessarily accompanied by any other spectacular qualities, I became interested in the historical phenomenon of the femme fatale. I have taken notes on it all during my scholarly career, and someday I expect to write a monograph in which I will explore the strange impact of beautiful women on otherwise honorable and sensible men. Not that I blame the women. My mother used to say, 'beauty is as beauty does.' I am merely amazed that other men have had to learn in even harder ways than I that my mother was right."

By then Sheila had pulled up to the parking place near her apartment, which also was as near as one could get to the Canon's house by car. She turned off the car, removed the key from the ignition and, turning toward him, said, "And now I've got to start learning that, too. I sure do appreciate your help."

Frank drove the Canon along the main street going south from the business district in Crawfordsville, past the several blocks devoted to stores and offices, and into the next section mainly occupied by what once had been the town's most elegant homes from the turn of the century to the depression. Although these houses had been relegated to less prestigious occupants in current times, they had not lost all their former glory. One of these aging beauties, set well back from the street on a corner lot with a wide circular driveway leading under a substantial porte-cochere, could have been a leftover from *Gone With the Wind*. It was a large white frame building in the Greek Revival style, complete with four fluted Ionic columns supporting the pediment of the roof that covered the first- and second-floor porches. Its recycled use was proclaimed by a sturdy sign standing on the front lawn; white lettering and neon tubes traced the words "Wellman Mortuary" on a base of cobalt blue enamel.

After Frank had neatly berthed the car within white lines painted on the driveway for that purpose, the Canon got out, went up the steps, crossed the porch over the green indoor-outdoor carpeting, and entered through French doors. Inside the door was a sign on a stand that told in removable letters whose remains could be viewed in which parlor. Ignoring that, he walked down the hall to the door marked "Office." Finding no one at the outer desk, but seeing light from under the heavy walnut door leading to an inner office, he knocked at what gold letters on the door proclaimed to be the sanctum of A. Courtney Wellman.

The man who opened the door was average height, slim without being thin, and possessed white wavy hair not much lighter than the color of his skin. His light blue eyes were set off by a dark suit, its lapel displaying the enameled pin of a service club adorned with a diamond. While the soft hand extended to Bothwell did not feel embalmed, neither did it feel capable of irreverence toward one who was.

"Come in, Canon Bothwell. What a pleasant surprise! I do hope that you have not come on business, or at least not on mine."

"No, Mr. Wellman, I do not have to make any arrangements, I am glad to say. I'm relieved to find you here on a Saturday afternoon."

"I had a few details to attend to when my secretary would not be around to interrupt me. I hope you have come because you have finally decided to sell me your car." Mr. Wellman smiled while offering to Bothwell a walnut visitor's chair upholstered in leather.

"No," said the Canon, sitting on the chair. "I am not ready to do that," he said, forbearing to add that he never would be. Recalling his gaze from the richly paneled walls decorated by little other than an oil-tinted photographic portrait of Wellman's father, the founder of the firm, several certificates and awards from a mortuary professional association, and a framed motto from a service club, Bothwell looked directly at his host and said, "I am afraid I have come on a much less pleasant mission."

Walking to his own chair, Wellman sat down, his face now serious.

"Mr. Wellman, let me assure you of the absolute privacy in which I intend to hold what I have to say to you. I have no intention of ever doing anything that would cause you any embarrassment, and if crucial matters having to do with the welfare and future of another person were not at stake, I would never presume to broach with you the unpleasant subject I now must raise."

Wellman grew, if possible, several shades whiter, but he maintained control, saying, "Canon, I am certain that you would never do anything to hurt anyone, if it could be avoided."

Crossing his legs and making a tent of his fingers in front of his chest, Bothwell said, "You are very generous, Mr. Wellman. To get to the point, I am looking into the death of one of our students, Mr. Seymour. I'm aware that you knew him, because I had the painful duty of sorting through his papers for his parents, and I discovered among them several letters from you. While the letters represent the soul of discretion, I have arrived at an interpretation of them on the basis of other information acquired about Mr.

Seymour. Let me assure you once again of the strict confidence in which I intend to hold this conversation."

Bothwell paused to let Wellman absorb his words. "Now let me share with you my interpretation of that correspondence. Mr. Wellman, I believe that young Mr. Seymour led you on to the point that you made a homosexual advance to him under the impression that it was expected and desired. His response, however, was to treat your behavior as an occasion for blackmail. I would be very grateful if you would tell me if my interpretation is correct."

Wellman's hand trembled, and he spoke with difficulty. "I am afraid that it is correct, Canon Bothwell. I am more ashamed than I can say, but that is exactly what happened. And I paid. The sums were not really exorbitant, and a breath of scandal would ruin our business in this town. You can imagine how discreet I have always been. There's never been any gossip in the fifty-eight years I've lived here."

"I am sure that is true, Mr. Wellman. Now I must ask you the question that is most relevant to my investigation: did you yourself have, or do you know of someone who did have, an appointment with Mr. Seymour on the evening before he died?"

"No, sir, I did not. When I discovered what an evil young man he was, I determined never to spend any more time in his company. As for others, I have no idea. I've never associated with the small local group of active homosexuals. Aside from the damage to the business that could result, their way of life is not mine. So I am unable to help you."

Bothwell nodded. "I thought that probably was the case. I rather imagine that he was with someone from Indianapolis, but I did have to look into every possibility. I am very grateful for your willingness to discuss what must be an unpleasant subject, Mr. Wellman." He rose to his feet, holding out his hand to Wellman.

"Thank you and good day."

Wellman took the Canon's outstretched hand and said, "Thank you, Canon Bothwell, for your promise to keep my grubby secret. I hope you do not think too harshly of me."

# 14

All Saints did not own a rectory, the original one next to the church having been torn down ages ago to make room for the parish house. When Father O'Grady came to Indianapolis, he knew that if his ministry in the inner city was to be effective, he had to live with his people. It was always tricky for a person with upper-middle-class education and tastes to know where to draw the line. On the one hand, identification with one's parishioners was an absolute necessity. On the other hand, one needed to be able to transcend the community, to set it in a wider perspective. The problem was not consumer goods as such, both because the ghetto had a degree of respect for certain kinds of status symbols, and also because the shoddiness of many of them added one more to the long list of question marks that one had placed beside the economic system producing them.

No, the problem was that one had come to enjoy books, pictures, and music. How can you remain true to these experiences of value—experiences that had a lot to do with your desire to come into the ghetto in the first place—without either creating barriers between yourself and others through tastes foreign to theirs or by the tiniest vestige of an assumption that your tastes made you in some way superior to those among whom you exercised your ministry?

When O'Grady first arrived at All Saints, the question had been simple to deal with because he was a bachelor at the time. An apartment in a nice building that had recently gone black worked fine. After his marriage, however, he and his wife bought a house in a middle-class neighborhood within the parish vicinity, a neighborhood that had been home to black professionals for some years. It was a roomy, two-story place in which people could stretch out and feel at home. One could sink into the furniture with a sense of security, and the host and hostess were there to do anything the furniture failed to do in the way of relaxing their guests.

When Roderick Bothwell rang the doorbell at four o'clock that Saturday afternoon, he had to wait a couple of minutes for it to be answered. Then the door opened, and Father O'Grady stood there facing him, dressed in his white neckband shirt with collar open, his clerical black trousers, and black-stockinged feet, holding a can of Stroh's in his hand.

"What's the matter, Rod, don't believe in rest for the wicked?" he asked as he urged his friend to enter and began to help him off with his hat and coat. "Come on back to the den and join me in my Saturday afternoon vice. I prop myself up in front of the tube with a cold brew and watch the *Wide, Wide World of Sports*. I don't really know what the draw is for me, since I've always been able to rise above any jock inclinations I may have ever had. But I find something very restful about watching all those people getting themselves in such a sweat, when all I have to do is to lie back in a recliner and observe them."

By the time his speech had ended, they had reached the den, and O'Grady switched off the large console color set. He re-ensconced himself in his chair, popped the top off a can of beer, passed it to his guest, and waved him to the sofa. "Sit down, Rod, sit down. I have about forty-five minutes before I have to go over to the church, plop myself down in the box, and see if I've put enough fear of God in any poor sinner this week to rate a confession or two to listen to. If that's what you've come for, I will even shrive you on my own time. What are friends for?"

"As salutary as that would undoubtedly be, Jamie, it is not about my own sins that I have come. You and I have talked about the death of Sebastian Seymour. I'm looking into the matter on behalf of the suspect, another student who, I believe, was not the perpetrator of the crime. According to the best information I can get, our Mr. Seymour used narcotics and was planning to induce others also to use them. Yet his source of supply was not in the Crawfordsville area. Indeed, I have been given reason to believe that he purchased them from a dealer in this section of Indianapolis. I am here in hopes you can provide me with leads by which I can follow up on that possibility."

O'Grady took a long swig of his beer. "Oh, Rod, fools do rush in! But I'll tell you what I'm gonna do. While I'm fairly streetwise myself, detailed information about the traffic here is something I've been happier not knowing. But I do have friends and parishioners who know as much as you can know while still staying alive. Let me put out some feelers and get back to you on Monday. Here's what we have to do. Jenny is at the studio now and is going to feel deprived because she missed you. Come back after Evensong on Monday, stop here for a drink, and I'll buy each of you a steak."

He jumped up from his chair and walked back to the television console. "We've got a few more minutes before I have to go make like a priest. Let me broaden your horizons. You are always bragging about how the study of history has made you blasé about humanity. However, there is one form of human depravity for which even you are not prepared. I want you to see a roller derby."

Wade Bryant was sitting in the armchair in the Jones' living room drinking an after-dinner cup of coffee with Horace, who sat on the sofa. The sheriff still wore his uniform shirt and pants of dark brown twill trimmed in tan. His gold badge reflected light from the lamp on the table beside him. He had felt relaxed enough to hang his Sam Brown belt and holster over the newel post when coming in the front door two hours earlier. Horace, however, had changed into comfortable off-duty wear: long-sleeved plaid sport shirt, corduroy slacks, and Weejuns.

Beth came into the living room. Taking off her apron, she said, "Well, the dishes are done, and Marcille and Jimmy are asleep. You men sit here and solve all the problems of law enforcement. I am going to run down to the A&P. They've marked down the meat and produce because they don't want to hold it over the weekend, and I want to take advantage of the prices."

Wade stood up to his full six two and pushed back his cowlick of hair that had grayed to rose gold. "Beth, honey, I hate to see you rush off to do something else after you already cooked a big supper for us and cleaned up the kitchen. Can't I go make the rounds for you?"

Horace said, "Wade, the A&P started doing this after Gertrude died, and so you don't know that shopping for these Saturday night bargains is Crawfordsville's social occasion of the week. Beth gets to gossip with all her friends. It takes a mighty good show on *Saturday Night at the Movies* to get her to stay home with me. So don't you go depriving her of a good time."

"Sorry, I didn't know. But anyway, Beth, I do thank you for taking pity on an old widower like me. I don't know why my own cooking hasn't killed me already. And the cafés in this town serve up food worse than what I make myself."

"Well, Wade, Horace thinks I only invite you to get him in good with his boss. Don't tell him that we got a thing going." Standing on tiptoe, she placed a kiss on his wrinkled, freckled jaw, and then dashed to get her coat. A minute later she was out the door.

Settling back down, the sheriff said, "Horace, I think you're one of the few men I ever met who did about as well in the marriage market as I did."

"Yeah, Wade, I feel mighty lucky. Speaking of married men, I feel sorry for old Seth alone in those woods when he could be home in bed with that beautiful wife of his."

Sticking a cigarette in his mouth and cupping his hands to light it with a kitchen match in his outdoorsman's habit, Wade said, "Yeah, I guess so, but from what I hear, them woods might not be any colder than her bed. Anyway, it sure looks to me like she drove him to it."

"When do you think we're going to find him, Wade?"

"I don't know. We might not. I told the lieutenant we might as well stop the organized search. We've been at it four days with all the men we could spare and two helicopters as well. If we get him now, it'll only be by accident. I don't have any doubt that he's in Turkey Run, but it looks like he can hide out there indefinitely. It's too much territory to keep under surveillance. Maybe in the spring when the campers start coming in droves somebody will see him, but nine chances out of ten they'd think he was another camper. And, besides, if it got too crowded, he could probably go to some other part of the country by then. By letting his hair and his beard grow and putting on glasses, he could get so his own wife wouldn't recognize him if she wanted to. Someday, somewhere he'll slip up and we'll get him. But you're right, it does seem like a helluva life for him, living on the run like that, never knowing when somebody might spot you."

Clyde Peabody, the naturalist at Turkey Run, was a well-built man in his mid-forties. His toothbrush mustache still remained a rich chestnut brown, although the hair on his head had already turned to salt and pepper. Sunday afternoons were a time he reserved for his own interest in the park. In the winter he attended Sunday school and church at the Marshall Baptist Church in the morning. But during the big camping season, he attended services at the Log Church on the park grounds and did without the Men's Bible Class he enjoyed so much. Sunday nights were one of the most popular times for nature walks, and he divided up the duties for those with the Junior Rangers. The afternoons he kept for himself. He liked getting away from the trails where the tourists were and observing the wildlife that had drawn him irresistibly to Turkey Run as soon as he finished his studies at Purdue.

This afternoon he had taken trail #10 after he crossed the suspension bridge and followed it almost halfway to Camel's Back before he struck off on his own. There was a beaver dam he wanted to check on, and he wanted to examine tracks in what was left of the snow—there was always something to learn. He had gone less than a quarter of a mile when he came into a clearing on the southern slope of a hill. As he emerged into the open field and had a clear view of the ridge above him, he saw vultures circling the thicket at the top and diving down into it. He was glad they had found food, since the snow hid most of what the birds fed on, even though their eyes were sharp as binoculars. He decided he would go see what they had found. For years he had been collecting notes for a short book on the birds at Turkey Run, and he might learn something that would help. Besides that, he knew that the giant birds' keen sense of smell had sometimes led them to leaks in gas lines, and that the Indiana Power and Light pipeline was buried right along there somewhere. It couldn't hurt to check that possibility, too.

After crossing the clearing, he saw a break in the underbrush right under that big sycamore, and he headed toward it. As he drew nearer, he recognized the entry into the thicket of a trail used by deer to move from their bedding area to their feeding ground and back. At the trail entrance a reflection of the bright afternoon sun from something on the ground caught his eye. Walking over to see what it was, he picked up an aluminum hunting arrow. As soon as he saw the yellow and black bands painted around the feathered end of the shaft, he knew who had been hunting out of season. The four-bladed head and indeed all of the shaft and feathers were evidence of the lethal journey the arrow had taken through the animal's body. Looking at the ground, Clyde easily spotted the trail of blood left by the injured animal when it had turned to seek shelter back in the thicket. He had not followed the blood trail long before he could hear flapping sounds in the brush made by the vultures fighting over food. Walking closer, he saw four of them dividing the spoil of deer entrails like German butchers measuring out sausage. By then the crossing of the trails where the deer had fallen and been gutted was sodden with blood. Clyde began to work his way back to the clearing, carrying the arrow with him. As much as he hated to do it, he would have to call the sheriff, and he would come back with the dogs.

Horace Jones half trotted beside the sheriff as they followed Jerry Fuller and his two bloodhounds. Even though he had seen the dogs in operation several times before, he still hadn't been able to allow reality to triumph completely over myth. His idea of bloodhounds had been formed by *Uncle Tom's Cabin* until Jerry had told him that true bloodhounds hadn't been imported into this country until 1888, and that slave-owners had used dogs that were usually a cross between Cuban mastiffs and Great Danes, claiming to the slaves that they were bloodhounds in order to heighten their fear of capture if they ever tried to escape. Certainly the dogs always turned out to be smaller that he remembered them, being only a little over two feet high at the withers and weighing right at one hundred pounds apiece. Then, too, it always came as a surprise that they did not bay when they followed a scent. In sophomore lit in high school he had been required to memorize the first few lines of Scott's *Lady of the Lake*, the first poem he had ever enjoyed, and he had particularly liked the bit about "the deep-mouthed bloodhound's heavy bay / Resounded up the rocky way."

Edgar and Clarabelle hardly barked at all as they snuffed along, turning now and then to go back over the ground where they had been, but generally galumphing along on the thirty-foot leather leads Jerry had attached to their martingale harnesses. The least fierce animals in the world, Jerry said that they were far more likely to lick anybody they caught than to bite them. Which had been just as well, because law enforcement agencies had used the dogs more often to look for missing children than to chase desperate criminals. Fuller had admitted that the real reason he kept them was that they made wonderful pets, and he enjoyed competing in the field trials held by the Sleuth Hound Club in Indianapolis.

Horace and Wade had come as soon as they received Peabody's call, arranging by phone for Jerry to meet them at the office at Turkey Run, and then driving over to the edge of the trail above the south side of the suspension bridge. There Jerry let the dogs out of the pen built onto the bed of his pickup, and they followed the naturalist up trail #10 to the place where he had cut out to go cross-country. When they had arrived at the edge of the thicket where the arrow had been found, Jerry let the dogs smell Seth's coat that the sheriff had brought along for the purpose.

None of them could have known that Seth had succeeded in making the job difficult for the dogs through his efforts to escape detection by the deer. He had carefully washed in melted snow heated over his early morning fire and then rubbed himself down with cedar oil from his survival pack. While doing so, he remembered that the Green Berets had used German shepherds to sniff out Viet Cong until the enemy brightened up and began washing with American toilet soap. All of this meant that the scent of the seminarian who had worn the B-24 jacket brought by the sheriff was very different from the smell of the man who had killed the deer; but there was enough similarity for the dogs to follow. At first they had rushed into the woods to the blood-soaked patch of leaves where the buzzards had made their feast, and then they turned around and pulled Jerry out of the cover and into the clearing.

From that point on, their speed was determined more by the terrain than by anything else. Occasionally Jerry saw that their tails had begun to droop. At such times he took them back along the trail to the last place their tails had been erect and let them get the scent once again and hold on to it more carefully. These lapses occurred mainly when the trail took a sharp turn, and they had been cannonballing too fast to make the corner. It was all great sport, and the dogs were obviously having a wonderful time.

Thus the chase went very smoothly until the trail came to a stream. Its bed was solid limestone, and there was no way the eye could observe the path of someone who had walked in its waters. Jerry took the dogs up and down the water's edge on both sides of the creek as far as he could go in either direction. Going north, they found that the banks of the creek became a ravine. Its banks became progressively steeper on both sides, and it seemed impossible that anyone could have left the stream from there on.

Besides, it was getting toward dark, and it would be dangerous to wade any farther. Nor did there seem to be any reason to return the next day. The only progress they had made was having confirmation that Seth was hiding out in the park. Probably the one bit of new intelligence they had was that he now had enough meat to last him for weeks, and he would therefore have no need to take dangerous forays out of his hiding place. His capture seemed no closer than before.

# 15

Roderick Bothwell needed air. It had been a long meeting of the Committee to Increase Student Participation in Decision Making at the Clergy Training College. The purpose was one that he favored in general. After all, students were older and more mature now, they were a talented group of people with many good ideas, and they had more at stake in the quality of their training for ministry than anyone else—except, probably, their future parishioners. He did feel that the push right now was in part a matter of the spirit of the times, and in part a reaction to the Dean's determination to maintain control over all that happened at the seminary, however trivial. Indeed, the trivial seemed to occupy more of his attention than the significant, apparently because it was composed of issues that he could grasp, matters in which he could tell if he was getting his way. The debate had been acrimonious, the chair seats hard, and the room stuffy. A brisk walk around the chapel was needed to clear his head before Evensong.

As he emerged from the sidewalk along the School side of the chapel onto the parking lot, he was astonished to see Sheila getting out of a BMW sedan. The young man in the driver's seat was trying to delay her departure, placing a restraining hand on her forearm and speaking to her importunately. For some reason, he looked familiar to the Canon, who had begun to move toward the car in case his assistance was needed. Sheila, however, was showing that she was perfectly capable of taking care of herself by stepping out of the car, slamming the door firmly, and walking briskly toward the sidewalk alongside the chapel, away from the parking lot and toward the campus.

It was then that she noticed Bothwell. She ran up to him and said, "Please walk along with me. Your presence should discourage that pest."

"Will that be sufficient, or should something further be done?"

"Oh, that will do for the moment, and I won't let him get close enough to bother me again."

"Did he force himself on you?"

"Not really. I've known him for years, and I ride to work in Indianapolis in the same carpool with him. We went steady when he was a senior at Champaign, and I was a sophomore. The next year, when he had moved up to the law school, he was too good to date undergraduates. Crawfordsville is his hometown—his name is Schuyler Cranston—and when we moved here, he came out to welcome us and invited me into the carpool. He didn't get out of line in any way until after Seth escaped. Then he began to say that I needed somebody to protect me. I quickly saw that he was the main person I would need protection from. It seems that he had regretted throwing me over ever since, and that he's been carrying the torch for me all along."

"I thought he looked familiar. I must have seen him around town. Well, let me know if he bothers you again. I am sure we can find a way to discourage him, even though I am a bit old to play Telemachus to your Penelope." When Sheila asked what he meant, he explained the Homeric allusion, and they went into chapel in a more relaxed frame of mind.

It was not until Frank had driven him halfway to Indianapolis that he remembered one encounter that he'd had with Schuyler Cranston previously: he was the young man Bothwell had seen coming out of the library on the night that Sebastian was killed.

The restaurant in the old hotel on North Meridian was still regarded as one of the best in Indianapolis, admittedly no overwhelming claim, as Jamie O'Grady was saying to his guest there on Monday evening.

"Rod, you remember W.C. Fields' great line: 'You can get the best steak in the world in Omaha, Nebraska, but after you've eaten it you're still in Omaha, Nebraska'? The difference between Omaha and Indianapolis is that the beef is not as good in Indianapolis."

Bothwell sat back into a position more comfortable for his stomach. "I'm afraid I'm not much of a judge, Jamie. Katrina already knew a lot of German recipes handed down in her family, and she borrowed my mother's cookbook and copied out all her recipes by hand. That added to her repertoire not only the Southern cuisine of the Delta, but also the Creole dishes that my father had come to love when he was in Tulane. I am thus more accustomed to sauces and combinations than I am to beef by itself. Still, my filet was just the way I like it: seared on the outside and running on the inside. And now with this good coffee and excellent cognac, I feel no need to disparage our adoptive city. I do hope that the drill you are going through with your cigar means that you are ready at last to inform me of the results of your researches in my behalf, and that Jenny will excuse our interrupting this charming evening with the discussion of some sordid shop."

Jenny O'Grady, who looked like the fashion model she had been twenty years earlier, said, "You know me, Rod. I will only object if it ceases to be sordid enough."

Beaming with pride in his lovely wife, O'Grady said, "You see the corrupting influence of the media, Rod. How is a poor priest to bring uplift into the home when his wife has been seduced by the bright lights of the television studio? I always admired the Lutheran tradition of the pastor's wife whose only interests were *Kinder, Küche, und Kirche,* and here I find myself tied to this woman who is constantly making a public spectacle of herself."

Jenny, probably the best-known local TV personality and anchor of the evening news on the local NBC affiliate without a male counterpart, had a social commitment at least as strong as her husband's and had used her beauty and charm to trap politicians and partisans of special interests into damaging admissions on the air under the impression that they were explaining complexities about which she should not worry her pretty little head. She and O'Grady had met when she had first given up modeling for reporting, and they had both been investigating pricing differences between ghetto and suburban outlets for the same supermarket chain. Initially, they had been suspicious of one another and had worked hard at suppressing the strong mutual attraction they felt for fear that their principles would be compromised through an unholy alliance. When each learned that the other was suspicious of his/her commitment to the cause and was afraid of the corruption of the movement by the church/the press, they laughed all the way to the altar.

"But," O'Grady continued, "I did look into the matter and found out some interesting things. It seems that the Reverend Mr. Smith leads an even more complex emotional life than I imagined. He gets through the day on a combination of uppers and downers that would give a rock star vertigo. I hear that on the rare occasions he travels, he has to take an extra suitcase for all his pills. But he's not selfish—I will say that for him. Being a Christian man, he is, of course, opposed to the use of beverage alcohol in any form, but he has learned that you don't have to smoke or drink to have a good time. At some of the love feasts they have over at Brotherhood Church the members enjoy better living through chemistry without ever knowing that they have been zapped by anything other than the Third Person of the Trinity."

He leaned forward and lowered his voice.

"When our boy Sebastian worked for the Reverend Bob, he was purchasing agent and *Braumeister* for the pharmaceutical arm of their operations. And when you are dealing in that volume, you do not pay retail to your friendly neighborhood dope peddler, you go to the main man. In Speed City, USA, that means 'Blue Gum' Blailock, who manages most of the drugs, prostitution, numbers, and what have you in the ghetto. If you have never seen his pimpmobile, you have missed an automotive wonder greater than any in the museum at the 500 track. It's roughly three times as long as that kiddy car of yours, has gold paint and a gold-padded vinyl cabriolet roof, and the grill, bumpers, and hubcaps are fourteen-carat gold plate. I think he got the idea from seeing the Mercedes that Hitler had made for Eva Braun. Anyway, the word I get is that after Sebastian's break with Uncle Bobby, Blue Gum kept him on the preferred customer list for old time's sake."

"Are you suggesting that Mr. Blailock is a sentimentalist?"

"As long as it doesn't cost him anything, why not? I think he admired the honkey boy's enterprise; he wasn't shiftless like so many of them white-assed kids, y'know? But if Sebastian had ever posed the slightest inconvenience to Blue Gum, I have no doubt that Blue Gum would have done like Isaiah said God did: he would have shaved with a hired razor."

Raising his brandy snifter to his nose, holding it cupped in his hands, and inhaling the fumes released through their heat, Bothwell seemed to be trying to bring insight into his mind through his nostrils. After a long pause he said, "Jamie, I take it that it would be overwhelmingly difficult for me to arrange an interview with Mr. Blailock."

"Rod, you may wager your dulcet derrière that it would. And setting it up wouldn't be half as hard as completing it without acquiring a split personality in the process. Jo' momma didn't raise you to be no 'gator bait, boy."

Sipping his cognac, Bothwell said, "Then, Jamie, it looks like my essay in detection is at an impasse. I have discovered a number of reasons why someone may have wished for Mr. Seymour's death—the Brotherhood Church and its negative attitude toward apostates, Mr. Blailock and his commercial interests, some unknown person who was a victim of blackmail over homosexual advances, possibly others—but all of these are only possibilities. I do not have the authority to press my investigation. Perhaps a law enforcement agency might have the clout to elicit additional information, but there is no leverage by which anyone can be compelled to satisfy my curiosity."

He paused and thought for a few moments. "Perhaps what has been accomplished so far will be enough to raise reasonable doubt about Seth's guilt in the sheriff's mind and set him to investigating other possibilities. I don't know. At the moment I feel defeated. I feel that I have let the boy down. The only thing that can clear his name adequately is showing in an irrefutable way what actually caused Seymour's death, and I don't know where to begin to find that out, and I don't appear to have the means to discover it even if I knew how. I feel like I did when I was a young teenager, and some older boys offered to take me on a snipe hunt. I didn't know that it was an old prank and went along feeling that I had been admitted to their society. They took me out into the woods and gave me a burlap bag into which they said they would drive the snipe, but then they went home and left me holding the bag."

His friend looked across the table at him and said, "Rod, I know it's hard, but you aren't licked yet. I've got a hunch you are going to see this thing through. I don't know how, but I am certain you will. Anyway, I'll be slaving away over a hot altar in the morning at seven to put in a good word for your efforts."

The Canon also made the identification of Sebastian's killer his intention at the Eucharist the next morning, although he did it from his stall rather than as celebrant. He remained on his knees for sometime after most others had left the chapel, his hands clasped tightly over the ledge in front of him while his eyes were focused on eternity beyond the sanctuary lamp, the tablets of the law, and the wall behind them through which his gaze passed without lingering or even consciousness.

Eventually his concentration was diminished by an awareness of an additional object of his peripheral vision. When its presence began to be insistent for his attention, he turned and saw Pete Whiston standing unobtrusively across the aisle, obviously waiting for him, but unwilling to interrupt his prayers. Getting up and reverencing the altar, he turned and said, "Is there anything I can do for you, Mr. Whiston?"

Standing there in his carpenter overalls and cotton flannel shirt, Pete said, "I hope I didn't bother you, Father. I wouldn't want to call back anybody who was in the Spirit. It's just that David Tharp said you would want to know." His voice was soft and sounded as though it had travelled many miles to get there.

"Don't apologize for wanting to do me a favor, Mr. Whiston. What information do you have that Mr. Tharp thought I would like to receive?"

"Well, you know I room next door to him and Sebas . . . , where Sebastian used to live, and when we were all in the john last night getting ready for bed, he was asking if anyone knew who had given Sebastian a ride into Indianapolis on the night he died. He said you were very anxious to know because you are trying to get Seth off."

"Yes, I'd like to know that very much," the Canon said, hardly daring to hope that he was about to learn what had puzzled him so much.

"Well, I did. I belong to a prayer-and-praise group in Indianapolis that meets on Friday nights. I always go in, and so when Sebastian asked for a lift, I couldn't refuse him. Jesus said, 'Whomsoever shall compel thee to go a mile, go with him twain,' so I had to take him, although I don't like to ride with demons."

"Demons?" the shocked priest asked, "do you think Sebastian was a demon?"

"Sebastian? No, Father, he wasn't a demon, he had a demon. He was possessed," Pete said, explaining the matter to the professor the way that one would explain to a small child.

"Oh? How did you know?"

"Because I've got the gift of discernment, Father. I can recognize who is possessed. And, Father, you don't have to worry about Seth. He didn't kill Sebastian."

"Do you know who did?"

"Of course, Father. God did it. He struck him down. Just like hitting a gar over the head with a hammer if you land one, God struck him down."

"Did you see that happen?"

"No, Father, I wasn't anywhere around at the time, but that has to be what happened. Sebastian was so evil that God had to take him away before he could do any more damage."

Despairing of this line of questioning, the Canon went back to the original object of his curiosity. "Where did you take Mr. Seymour on that Friday night?"

Here the answer was straightforward. "I took him to that place he used to work, the Brotherhood Church."

"Did he say anything about why he was going there?"

"No, Father, he didn't say a word. Was that all you wanted to know? Breakfast is almost over."

Shaken by this abrupt shift between levels of reality, Bothwell let him go, greatly relieved to have something concrete to work on, but aware as well that Pete Whiston was in far worse shape than they had imagined, and that the faculty would have to devote some serious attention to his condition in the very near future.

Bothwell had only a nine o'clock class that morning, so by 10:30 he was able to make it to the office of the sheriff with whom he made an appointment by phone. Horace was waiting with his superior when the Canon arrived. Neither had been aware of the professor's competitive efforts at criminal investigation, and they listened with interest as he gave a complete account of his activities, and both looked genuinely disappointed when he concluded with the negative results of his detective efforts.

The sheriff responded by saying, "Well, Reverend, I never have known an amateur to get very far in efforts to solve a crime, although you'd be surprised at the number who have tried it right here in Montgomery County. I guess it comes from reading all those books. Anyway, I'll have to admit you've done a lot better than most. In fact, in all honesty I'll have to admit more than that. I'll have to say that you have been looking into a lot of things that I ought to have a go at. And I still will, especially after what you told me about the Seymour boy's going to Reverend Smith's place that last night. I just learned something the other day that might fit in with that, something that didn't seem related before."

Bothwell raised his eyebrows as Wade continued. "On that same night, or early the next morning to be exact, a Crawfordsville patrol car stopped a car coming into town on the Yountsville road. All it was being stopped for was a burnt-out headlight, but it looked for a minute like it wasn't going to pull over. But it did. When the driver came up to the squad car to ask what the trouble was, he was a big young black man, and he had on a uniform that looked like what you describe for those Soldiers of Christ. When he went back to his own car and opened up the door to get back in, the patrolman noticed three others in the car dressed the same way. Well, he took the license tag number and checked it with the State Police. The car was registered in the name of Reverend Smith.

"There's no doubt in my mind that you've made a strong case for other people having a motive to murder that boy in addition to young Clarke. But

I still have to say that knowing all those other motives doesn't convince me that Clarke didn't do it. There are two things that are hard to get around. The chewed match stem and other things can be explained away, but I don't know how to explain away the lack of any other footprints going up to that chapel, and I don't know how to overcome the virtual admission of guilt involved in his escape. The lie detector test didn't help any, but the footprints and the escape are what convince me he did it."

Bothwell had listened to the sheriff with great interest and then reflected quietly for a few seconds after the recital was over. "Sheriff, I have a good guess as to why he ran away, and I don't think that it had anything to do with the present case. I wish I could talk with him. I'm sure he would corroborate my interpretation."

"We almost caught up with him on Sunday. Too bad we didn't. Then you coulda asked him."

That was Bothwell's first news about the discovery of Seth's arrow where a deer had been killed. Eagerly he asked to be shown on a map where the trail had run out and how to get there from the highway. "Sheriff," he said, "I believe that I could get Seth to talk to me, if you would let me go out there by myself. I also believe that I could get him to write out his reason for running away. Will you trust me to try?"

"Reverend, you're a law-abiding citizen who has the right to go where he wishes without police harassment. If I was to hear that you was driving out Highway 47, I wouldn't have any reason to think that you were likely to consort with an escaped criminal. You're free to go where you like without any danger of pursuit from my office."

"Thank you, Sheriff. I appreciate your confidence more that I can say. And I also have an idea of how we might learn a little more about the Reverend Mr. Smith."

# 16

The hike back into the woods had been strenuous for Bothwell, who led a very sedentary life. Even though he walked enough to have some muscle tone, his walking was all on flat surfaces on the campus and mostly on sidewalks. He felt stiff when he had to raise a foot to advance up a steep incline, and he shifted weight from one foot to the other with a bit of uncertainty about how far to make it go. Stooping to go under limbs or brush made him regret anew the tendency of his scholar's body to weight. But he had not complained and had been able to follow the directions Wade had given him well enough. He had made what speed he could because he was convinced that he would need as many daylight hours as possible. Horace had warned him that when the sun vanished behind the tops of the trees in the west, darkness would come quickly.

The Canon sat on the log of an old beech tree that had fallen by the bank of the stream across a small clearing near where Seth's trail had ended. Among the many things that he did to fill the hours of waiting was to read the initials and names that scarred the trunk of the big tree. It brought back memories of his own Mississippi childhood when he too had gone into the woods and taken along a pocketknife. No bark was quite so easy to carve as the smooth surface of the beech. One did not even have to make deep incisions. It was enough to push the tip of the blade into the bark and watch the crumbly orange inner bark come trailing out ahead of the steel point. No wonder that beeches that had always been as remote as this one from the paths of people had seldom preserved their trunks illiterate. Who were the couples whose names had been linked in this way before the turn of the century? Were the liaisons real or merely the fantasy of their engraver? Had the couples married, reproduced, loved, fought, rejoiced, and suffered together? How long had they been in their graves, these men and women whose banns were so optimistically published here in this wooded glen?

Even though the temperature rose to the upper thirties by early afternoon, and most of the snow had melted, Bothwell was glad that he had dressed sensibly to go out, and that he had on long underwear as well as his overcoat, galoshes, muffler, fur-lined gloves, and hat. During his vigil he had walked around the small clearing to keep his blood circulating and to work off some nervous energy. And, as usual, when he found time on his hands with nothing to read and nothing to do, he thought. First he reviewed every aspect of the case and found every item in his memory labeled and filed, but no new insights came to him. He thought about the book on which he had worked for a number of years, which he would call *Sur le Pont: The Avignon Papacy as Bridge Between the Medieval and Modern Worlds*. It was to be a social history organized according to the occupational groups that made up the society, and it would have the various sections introduced by the appropriate verse from the French nursery rhyme. In thinking of this, he did decide that his material on Petrarch was getting too voluminous to be included in this work, and thus it would require a separate book of its own. He did, after all, have sufficient original insight there to warrant yet another book on the subject, although he did wish that scholars would show more restraint about publication.

As he waited, he took from his pocket the orange he had stopped by the grocer's to purchase. As soon as he arrived, he had lunched on the hard rolls and cheese with which he had also provided himself, but now he was as interested in leaving a sign of his presence as he was in nourishment. Seth had commented on his Mercator projection orange peel when he had come over for counsel on his term paper. If he found one here, he would know who was looking for him. The orange eaten, he lay the peel near the stream in what he hoped would be an obvious place and squatted down to wash the stickiness of the fruit from his hands in the icy water. Then he returned to his seat on the beech trunk to make explicit the prayer that hung in the wings of his consciousness from the moment that he had heard that Seth's trail had been found.

By the time that he had finished, the sun had reached the point where its bottom edge was slightly penetrated by the tips of the tallest trees. It was time for him to be heading back and call it a day. He thought gratefully that Frank in his ingenuity would have found a way to keep the interior of the big car warm without running the risk of poisoning himself on carbon monoxide.

Even though Bothwell had been impressed with the cogency of recent Vatican pronouncements suggesting that so strict a fast was not necessary before receiving Holy Communion, he had not changed his own practice because returning home after the Eucharist for a leisurely breakfast with the morning paper was such a satisfactory way to begin the day. The next morning, however, he had asked Katrina to get up early and prepare him both a hearty breakfast to be consumed on the premises before he went to chapel and also a lunch and thermos of coffee to go. Putting these in his brief case, he asked Frank to place a couple of cans of motor oil in a string orange bag, put a beer can opener in the brief case, and meet him with the car behind the chapel after the service. On the way down campus he stopped by the School, went to his classroom and wrote on the blackboard that he would not meet any of his classes that day, leaving instructions about profitable ways in which hours thus liberated could be employed.

When they arrived at Turkey Run, he had Frank drive him by the office where he told the Property Manager, Lloyd Hall, that he was going to try to establish contact with Seth, and that the sheriff was aware of his intention and had made no objection. In order to inform Seth of his presence, he wanted to build a signal fire. He took the precaution of asking permission, both because he did not wish to alarm the park personnel, and also because he did not want any of them invading the area to put out a forest fire at what could be a crucial moment. Hall not only agreed completely to all of his stipulations but even gave him a small bundle of kindling to place with the oil in the orange sack, because getting a fire started with all the wood so wet from melted snow could develop into quite a job.

By the time he had lugged his supplies back to the clearing on the stream bank, gathered wood, built a fire, and mounted a thick column of black smoke by pouring the oil on the wood and laying branches with wet leaves on top of the fire, it was mid-morning. Having gathered enough fuel to keep the flame fed most of the day, he settled back to enjoy its cheery blaze, grateful that there was little breeze to prevent the smoke from rising straight. This time he had come prepared, and so he drew from his pocket a small leather-bound copy of the *Divine Comedy* and settled on his beech log seat to enjoy the mellifluous Italian of Dante, knowing that his attention would be held and entranced as long as he was able to read.

Lunchtime came and went. Katrina did know how to provide for the inner man. Thick slices of homemade whole wheat bread were filled with a slab of meatloaf. A hard-boiled egg, some carrot and celery sticks, and a crisp, tart Jonathan apple were exactly what was needed to top off the sandwich. The coffee had been laced with just enough brandy to course warmly through his bloodstream without being in the least soporific. A little adjustment of the fire, and he was ready for Dante again.

About two-thirty he heard his name called and looked around to see Seth standing back in the woods beyond the edge of the clearing. "Hello, my boy. I am grateful to you for coming. It is safe for you to come out—I am quite alone, and I am unarmed."

"I knew it was you. I found your orange peel early this morning when I was out for exercise and gathering a few plants for a salad. When I saw the smoke, I gave everything in the woods time to settle down, and then I began to circle around to be sure that you were alone. I saw your driver waiting by the edge of the road. I suppose the arrow I lost was what put the sheriff on the track and allowed him to trace me this far?"

"Yes, it was, although he had no confidence in his ability to get any closer to you. If he did, I don't suppose that he would have ever consented to lean on a broken reed like me.

"Seth, I'm sorry to report that I have not yet succeeded in clearing your good name, so I think it is best for you to remain in hiding a while longer, but I do believe that some progress is being made. At least the sheriff is now willing to consider some possibility other than that you killed Mr. Seymour, and that is a beginning. One of the reasons he is still rather convinced that you are probably guilty is your escape, which he considers to be a tacit admission of guilt. But that is not why you ran away, is it?"

"No, Canon, I simply panicked. It had been just a little over six months since I had escaped after two years imprisonment in Vietnam. Being in jail gave me an overwhelming sense of being back there, and I just couldn't stand it. You know, when you see the movies or read the novels, no one ever cracks under torture, but all of us POWs did to some extent, although I'm glad to say that I heard of only three who ever went over to the enemy or even helped them very much. But if they wanted you to do some little thing, they could usually make you do it. We felt that it was by giving in before it got too tough that we got the leverage to avoid compromising what would really help them. But it's hell living under those circumstances, and I couldn't get over the feeling that I'd been thrown right back into the pit. When anyone started interrogating me, I would break out in a cold sweat, and when that Asian guy was administering the lie detector test, I thought I would go out of my skull."

"That's about what I thought had happened. I want you to write that out for me so that I can give it to the sheriff. He wants to believe you're innocent, and we have begun to get him to consider that possibility seriously. I think this will help. Here, use my note pad."

While Seth was writing, Bothwell went on to say they still had the problem of only Seth's and Sebastian's tracks in the snow around the chapel. In order to show that someone else was guilty, they would have to explain that. Meanwhile, he thought it was best for Seth to stay low in Turkey Run. When Seth had handed the pad back to him, he read over what had been written and said, "That will do very well. Now, we need to think about a signal I can use the next time I want to see you. Something you can respond to immediately."

"Yeah, that sounds like a good idea. It needs to be something that I hear rather than something that I see so that I can't miss it."

"While I haven't shot a gun since I was in college, I do think that makes the only sound we could count on to carry far enough. I still have my father's sidearm, a Browning automatic, and Frank has kept that oiled. Why don't we say that when you hear three shots fired in rapid succession, you will come running? And if I fire five shots, you will know that you have been exonerated, and that you can go home a free man."

"Three's the traditional distress signal, but you're beginning to make it sound like beautiful music, and five will sound like the heavenly choir."

"That reminds me of one other thing I wanted to tell you. Since you have been gone, I have come to know your wife rather well, and I can assure you that she loves you very much and is very concerned for your safety."

The young man's face behind its week-and-a-half's growth of beard lightened instantly, and much of the tightness at the corners of his eyes and mouth vanished. "Canon, that's almost the only good news I have had since I've been back in the States." Then the look of gloom returned, and he said, "But I would still make a lousy husband, even if I get out of all this. I told you what I'm like with women."

"Yes, son, and I want to say now what I did not get a chance to say then. Let me begin by telling you that I understand, because in many ways my upbringing was very similar to yours, with one crucial difference.

"I was also brought up as an only child by a mother with whom I was very close. I did not even have your natural athletic ability to pull me into more masculine circles. Instead, I was bookish and found my defense mechanisms in an aptitude for scholarship. My mother was a very strong woman, and it was easy to share her aesthetic interests. And she was lonely and depended on my company about as much as I depended on hers.

"The difference, however, was that she and my father had been deeply in love. He perished leading his regiment in an attack on German trenches at Chateau Thierry. A relation such as they had was a hope that my mother always cherished for me, and she encouraged me to think that deep love between a man and a woman expresses itself sexually and physically. Because of my own foolishness and shyness, I have never known the fullness of that relation myself, but I am convinced that it is a real possibility for you if you can get over your shame about your feelings for Sheila and recognize that your body can mean as much to her as hers does to you. Give her a chance."

Sitting at one end of the long table in the meeting room at the offices of the Heil Foundation, the Reverend Bob Smith looked uncomfortable, as though sitting down in a circle with others as a peer was not his way of interacting with people. He seemed to miss his pulpit—the monopoly on attention that it gave him, and the opportunity it afforded for spellbinding. At times as he addressed the group, his voice would rise above the conversational tones and begin to take on a hammering, hectoring quality of demagoguery. His blond pompadour was lacquered against displacement by the jutting of his chin and the twisting of his neck, but his light green eyes would lose at times their focus on the people at the table and appear to be captured by dreams and visions invisible to the others present. Committee meetings were not his métier.

Yet obviously the success of the present one was very important to him. His latest drive was to get massive draft counseling assistance for the ghetto because, as he pointed out, one of the effects of the peace movement as it existed was racist. The young men who were burning their draft cards, shouting "Hell no, we won't go," and heading to Canada were white college students, the children of affluence and privilege. That meant that an even larger percentage of those who were drafted and sent off to fight and die would be black. Young black men had so little stake in the society that they could not even opt out. They needed a way of learning how to avoid fighting a white man's war of aggression against an exploited non-white people seeking self-determination.

Funding such a program, however, would take money, white money ironically, and Heil money to be specific. As one of the largest foundations in the country and as the only one that combined emphases on community service, religion, and Indiana, the Heil Foundation was obviously the only place to go for the money that was needed. But those Heil honkies insisted that such things be ecumenical in sponsorship, and Smith had to convince a roomful of representatives of mainline churches that they wanted to endorse and sponsor his program if he was going to get the money for it. That was an uphill fight. Many of them had enough questions about him already, and the prevailing spirit of Indianapolis was not New Left, as a quick look at the editorial pages of local papers would show.

When he finished the basic presentation of his case and asked for questions, he was relieved to see that they began mildly, indicating only the curiosity after details of a basically sympathetic audience. When Dr. Bothwell began to make throat-clearing noises, move his chair around, and hold out his hand in preparation for entering the discussion, Smith began to get nervous. He knew how much Bothwell's opinion was respected by the others present, and his staff had reported to him their success in keeping Bothwell out of his office a few days before.

When the question came, it could not have been more damaging: "Mr. Smith, you may remember that I am Roderick Bothwell, and that I represent the Department of Christian Social Relations for the Episcopal Diocese of Indianapolis. While I must say that I believe that you have made a good point and made it cogently, I must also say that I have some peripheral concerns. My questions do not concern the program you propose so much as they concern the administration of it by your group. I am aware that there is at Brotherhood Church a para-military organization called the Soldiers of Christ. I know of many good services that this group has performed in the past, but I also have information about recent changes in its course of study and drill practices that cause me concern. And I have some questions about the spread of their activities beyond the city; I hear a detachment of them were on a mission in Montgomery County week before last . . . "

Smith knew what dangerous ground they were on. Nothing scared these whites so much as seeing blacks appear to have power that they were not afraid to use. It had been an error to have two sergeants to run interference for him today like bodyguards and to take stations on either side of the door when he had entered the meeting room. But what was Bothwell saying now? He may be offering to let him off the hook. " . . . but since these are probably purely personal concerns, I suggest that we not take up the time of the group. When our committee adjourns for lunch in the cafeteria here, perhaps you and I can take our trays into an empty room and deal with these issues privately."

When they were alone Bothwell went straight to the point. "The real questions I want to ask you are those I would have asked the other day in your office if I had been permitted to see you, but they have become more specific now because I have additional information. The first concerns the visit Mr. Seymour made to you on the night he died. Don't bother to deny it. I have a witness who saw him. What did he want?"

"What he usually wanted, to put the squeeze on me by threatening to expose me."

"How did you respond?"

"By having him kicked out. I have a mission from God to perform. I can't waste my time on pipsqueak turncoats. He is an apostate and we have delivered him to Satan."

"What do you mean by that?"

"We kicked him out of the church. Now he can have no part of our kingdom. Now he'll burn in hell."

"But you left the means of his going in the hands of God, you did not . . . er, hasten him along?"

"Of course not. You can't prove that we're mixed up in anything like that."

"Then why were four of your Soldiers of Christ near where he was killed just after his death?"

"I thought we needed to know where he lived, and how to get around out there for future reference. But it didn't pay off. These city kids got scared out there in the country so much on whitey's turf. They didn't even get out of the car."

"You've given me the answers I wanted, and I think that I accept them. Thank you. But while I will support Heil funding for draft counseling centers in the ghetto, I am going to propose that they be under the administration of the Fellowship for Reconciliation or some such ecumenical group rather than your church. Good day, Mr. Smith."

# 17

On Friday Roderick Bothwell did nothing toward solving the mystery of who killed Sebastian Seymour. So much of the week had been devoted to investigation that the duties he was hired to perform had begun to accumulate and demand attention. After he went to sleep that night, however, he discovered that his mind was preoccupied with questions related to the crime. Normally he slept quite soundly and, even on the rare occasions when he did not, he had learned to be calm in the face of his sleeplessness. Some of his clearest thinking had been done at three o'clock in the morning. That was not the way it was on this Friday night. He tossed and turned, never fully asleep nor fully awake. The questions had an insistent, nightmarish quality. On the threshold of consciousness they would become so loud and demanding that he would have to wake up; but once awake he discovered that his mind had no new data to reflect on, that nothing had been cast up by the unconscious. He could not remember a similar night since he had come down with feverish flu on the night after he had seen Hitchcock's film, *The Birds*.

Despairing of rest, he rose early, dressed, and went to the chapel. He did not think of it then as the scene of the crime, but only as the place where his mind could find rest. He had been in his stall on his knees for most of an hour when the sacristans arrived to begin the final preparations for the morning services. He was only dimly aware of the two students in their cassocks moving about the chapel, placing vessels on the credence table and altar, setting Bible and missal markers at the day's lections, laying out vestments, and performing the other little chores that needed to be done for services to run smoothly.

Since it was Saturday, there were also the weekly tasks to be performed. Fred Andrews came out of the sacristy carrying the short pole with a hook on the end that was used to lower the sanctuary lamp so that the seven-day candle could be changed. In his other hand he held a replacement candle in its glass jar that looked for the world like a king-size jelly glass. As the hook on the pole was caught in the molded opening for it on the bottom of the heavy brass lamp and the lamp was pulled down on its chain, its counter-weight pod rising simultaneously like that of an elevator, something about the action caught Bothwell's attention, and for the first time his conscious-ness dealt with the activity of the sacristans as its object.

Already people were beginning to come in for the service, and so it was too late to do anything then. Bothwell, who was normally quite recol-lected for the liturgy, found himself as distractible as a four-year-old that morning; he could hardly wait for the dismissal. As soon as it came, he grabbed a startled librarian and asked him if he had a strong magnifying glass in his desk drawer. Within seconds he had pulled him into the library, taken the glass, returned to the sacristy, grabbed the sanctuary lamp rod, lowered the lamp, and was inspecting its bottom when an amazed Fred Andrews came out to begin his cleanup after the service.

"Fred," the Canon said, "call the sheriff's office quickly, and tell Deputy Jones that I want him out here immediately with all of his crime lab equip-ment. Tell him that I have discovered the weapon that killed Sebastian Seymour."

Horace's examination of the lamp produced a minute strand of fiber, two long blond hairs, and a few cells of skin tissue. Later when the results came back from the lab it was clear that the fiber matched the wool of Se-bastian's poncho, the hair was identical with that of the deceased, and the tissue came from human skin. The little that could be determined from such a small tissue sample was consistent with its having come from the back of Sebastian's neck. Already, though, what had happened was pretty obvious. After Seth had left the chapel, Sebastian had come in and engaged in the devotions that Fred Andrews had observed on other occasions and described as "strange gyrations in front of the altar," and "a deep bow, mov-ing from side to side." Someone had pulled the lamp back and let it fly with enough force against the back of Sebastian's neck to sever his spinal cord.

The Canon and Horace agreed that the use of the sanctuary lamp as a weapon suggested very strongly that the murderer was a member of the CCTC community rather than an outsider such as one of the Soldiers of Christ or Schuyler Cranston. They were still no further along than ever on having any idea of how the murderer left the chapel without leaving footprints in the snow. Meanwhile, though, the Canon thought they ought to be able to figure out a little more about how the murder was actually committed.

"The first question," he said, "is whether the murderer stood beside Mr. Seymour and pulled the lamp down with the rod. On the whole, that seems very unlikely. Surely the presence of someone beside him in the dark chapel engaging in such an activity as trying to hook the rod into the lamp and give it a good jerk down would have distracted Seymour enough to rouse him out of the vulnerable position. How else could it have been done?"

Stepping back to survey the situation, Bothwell grasped his chin thoughtfully. In the stillness of the chapel it seemed as though his great domed brow was throbbing with thought. "Some sort of twine must have been used. Perhaps it could have been anchored from in front by being tied around the altar rail and then passed through the eye for the hook in the bottom of the lamp. Somebody sitting in a back pew could have held the cord and yanked down on it at the proper time. Fred Andrews mentioned to me once that the lamp comes down very easily. Horace, you didn't find any heavy string or anything of that sort when you searched the chapel, did you?"

"We didn't find anything nearly so long as you are talking about, but one thing did surprise us. We did discover a piece of monofilament fishing line, four or five inches long. It was pretty heavy stuff, too, about twenty-pound test. It was kinda gnarled up—you know the way it gets. But we didn't figure out any explanation for it and decided that it probably didn't have anything to do with the murder. Most of the stuff we found didn't."

"Heavy fishing line, that reminds me of something . . . but I can't think what. If it's important, I guess it will come to me, although whether in three minutes, three hours, or three days, I cannot say. Meanwhile, I suppose you will want to call the sheriff. Why don't you come up to my house to do that, and then we can talk about this a little more."

When Horace returned from the phone call, Bothwell no longer looked confused, but he did look distressed. "I think I understand it all, now. Come with me back to the chapel, and I think I can explain it."

Walking down campus he remained silent and remote, but once they entered the chapel, he immediately became businesslike. "Now, Horace, if I'm right, we will find either a wood staple or an eye screw or the holes or hole from which one has been removed. One of the faculty stalls nearest the center—the Dean's or my own—seems most likely, but it could have been the end of one of the student pews, probably that of a Junior."

A diligent search for twenty minutes produced no results, but then Horace, who had a capacity for seeing the obvious, said "Canon, could it have been this?" and pointed to the ring on the outside end of the Dean's stall where the Dean's staff of office could be locked into place.

"It very probably was, Horace. Now come with me." Bothwell led him out into the narthex and up the stairs to the organ loft. In addition to the console, the loft also contained some old pews in which a choir could sit when special music was performed. Going to the front one, he moved along the rail until he came to the spot directly behind the Dean's stall. Pointing down, he said, "See how much more controlled the descent of the lamp would have been if the murderer had his line go through a fixed point down there and did his pulling from up here. I think the fall would have been straighter and the force harder this way. Besides, one could see when the neck of Mr. Seymour was in the right place, and there would be less risk of being spotted by the victim."

"All right, now come over here," the Canon continued as he strode energetically toward the round window on the west wall. The window, which was over a yard in diameter, had small steel rods attached to its back on its horizontal axis. These rods allowed it to pivot open on hot days when ventilation was needed in the loft. Bothwell opened the latch at the top of the window and swung the window open. "Now, Horace, I am going over to the Green Building, and I will open the window there at the end of the hall on the second floor. When you see me do that, I want you to slip out of this window and lower yourself onto the roof of the arcade stretching between these two buildings. I think the task will be neither difficult nor dangerous to you."

After Bothwell opened the window in the other building, and Horace had made his crossing and justified the Canon's confidence in the ease of the effort, Bothwell continued his explanation. "When you searched the chapel after Seymour's death, I doubt that you looked out the loft window. If you had, you probably would have seen nothing to make you suspicious since the crossing was made before much snow had fallen, and the pattern of the snow on the arcade roof would have been irregular because of its exposure to the wind.

"I think it would be far better for me alone to confront the person who made that crossing. I want you to go downstairs and wait for me in the refectory. No, no, I'll be all right. We are far less likely to have another unfortunate incident if we do it this way."

The fiddler inside the door at the end of the hall had begun to play about the time that Bothwell had opened the window. When he had looked across from the other side of the arcade, he thought he could see a figure standing back from the window and watching what was going on. The music had no tune in the ordinary sense, and yet it was filled with more feeling than the priest could remember in any of the compositions of the masters. The music was sad; it enunciated clearly a longing that must have been hitherto inexpressible. Somehow wild agony and the nobility of tragic suffering were held together in a paradox of sound. The playing continued as Bothwell opened the door and went in and sat quietly on the end of the bed. It continued for sometime and then ended suddenly on a shrieking discord that Bothwell thought must have been the way the Temple veil sounded when it was rent in twain.

The hand holding the bow flipped down to the side of its owner and lay there inert, almost catatonic. Pete Whiston's round blue eyes continued for a while to gaze over distant horizons. And then the boy sat down.

After several more minutes of silence, he looked up at his professor and said softly, "You know."

"Yes," the answer came back. "I know."

"I thought God told me to do it."

"I had assumed so."

"Will they lock me up?"

"I imagine that they will put you in a hospital."

"Will they take my fiddle away from me?"

"I am sure they will want you to keep it. They will recognize how important it will be in helping you to get well. Are you ready to go now?"

"Yes."

Early that afternoon the Canon made a phone call. "Sheila, my dear, this is Roderick Bothwell. I know that it is still quite brisk outside, but I wonder if you are free to humor a whim of mine and take a walk in the woods. I have something I want to show you."

When she expressed her ability and willingness to do so, the priest then asked if he could impose further by asking her to take her car. There being no difficulty with that either, they agreed that she would pick him up in half an hour.

In the car he said little about the effort to exonerate Seth. About the only thing connected with the case that he mentioned was his discovery that Schuyler Cranston had been almost as jealous over her plans to go on the weekend retreat with Sebastian as Seth had; he had even come out to the campus that night with some vague idea of finding out what was going on, but when he arrived on campus he realized that he did not know where to go, whom to see, or what to do. After wandering into the library and looking around, no better idea came to him; and so he went home feeling silly, apparently a rare state for him.

The nearest thing to a subject the Canon seemed interested in discussing was a field sport he had enjoyed in his Mississippi youth—snipe hunting. When Sheila said that she had never hunted at all and had never spent much time in the woods until Seth had taken her to Turkey Run on their honeymoon, Bothwell dropped the subject, saying only that it was in Turkey Run that he wanted to walk. The rest of the conversation was desultory and charming, the kind of light and comfortable chitchat that seemed appropriate to a Saturday afternoon outing in the woods.

After bypassing the main entrance to the park and driving closer to where all its trails had their beginnings, Bothwell instructed her to park by the side of the road. From there, they set out on a hike that was more than a mere stroll. In fact, it was more rugged than any of the marked trails in the park, although some of them can make fit people pant. Eventually, they found themselves in a little clearing by a creek, situated just before the creek entered a ravine that it had cut over the centuries through steep limestone banks.

Sheila stopped to catch her breath, sitting down on a large beech log that lay across the clearing. In the next instant she was amazed to see Bothwell reach into his overcoat pocket, draw out a Browning service automatic, point it to the sky, and pull the trigger five times rapidly. He then placed the gun back in his pocket and said to her, "There will be someone here soon that you want to see. Frank has followed us in my car, and I will leave now to go back with him. In the future you'll be able to say that you have been on a snipe hunt, and it was the nicest one of all."